Conniving Attraction

Destinee Boston

For all the girls that live in their head

Prologue

My sister and I have never gotten along, truly. From a young age we were constantly fighting for space, attention, and resources, like two male hamsters in a cramped cage.

I felt as though there was never enough room for the both of us to exist in this small world. That only one of us could make it out alive.

I always knew it was going to be *me.*

1

Karma

I'VE ALWAYS HAD dreams of being someone else. Someone prettier, richer, and more popular than I was, ever since I was a little girl. Occasionally, when I'm by myself, I like to pretend that I am.

Last night, while packing my bags, I made a promise to myself: to embrace new experiences, make friends, have fun, and stop overthinking everything. In high school, I struggled to maintain friendships, by always overanalyzing every situation. This time, I vowed to do things differently. I was so excited about the move that I barely slept. Early in the morning, as my taxi pulled up, my mom helped me load all my bags into the trunk.

Her face carried a sorrowful expression, and a pang of guilt settled over me for leaving her like this. But I'm happy I'm going. Now she knows how it feels. I feel like she won't really miss me anyway, she'll probably find a man to keep her company soon. I need to do this for myself.

After stepping off the plane in New York. My phone buzzes, and I glance down to see a message from him. I don't reply. Maybe I don't need to anymore. New York is brimming with people and possibilities.

As I make my way through the airport, I notice someone standing by baggage claim, holding a sheet of paper with my name on it. The email had mentioned an escort would meet me. I approach the man, who's dressed in a sharp suit.

"Hi! Thanks so much. I've never had an escort at the airport before—I feel like a celebrity or something!" I laugh nervously.

The man offers me a tight, polite smile and grabs my bags. "This way."

I follow him, and by the time we reach the car, his demeanor softens. He opens the door for me, loads my bags into the trunk, and smiles warmly.

Once we're both seated inside, he asks, "Where are you from?"

"Florida," I answer automatically. It's a lie.

I have no idea why I said that. His thick New York accent throws me off—it's sexy in a way that makes me nervous. *Wow, I can't believe I'm really here. I'm really doing it.*

"Are you excited to work at Introspection?" he asks, his hands steady on the wheel as we navigate the busy highway, surrounded by a sea of billboards, towering skyscrapers, and yellow taxicabs. It's just like I imagined.

I smile back at him, my excitement bubbling over.

"Yes! I'm so excited. This has been my dream for so long—to work for one of the biggest marketing companies in the world!"

He chuckles. "I've heard only a few people make it out alive."

His words catch me off guard. I tilt my head, confused.

"Not to scare you," he continues, "but I've been doing this every year, picking up new interns, and I barely see any of them stick around. So many people just vanish, and the company's always hiring replacements. It's like a revolving door."

I glance at him, unsure why he's telling me this.

He goes on, "People get competitive, cutthroat even. Eventually, you wonder if all this is worth it—lying, hustling to make a quick buck, all for some instant gratification, or to look good to a boss who doesn't really care about you. They just want you to make money for them."

I give him a skeptical look. "Did you used to work at Introspection?"

He looks over at me, his expression suddenly sharper, like he's been waiting for this question. "Yeah, back in my younger days."

"So, how do you think I can make it?" I ask, genuinely curious despite his ominous tone.

He smirks, tapping the steering wheel thoughtfully.

"If you really want this, stand your ground. They need strong personalities, people who won't be pushed around. I didn't know much about marketing when I started, but I had a backbone, and they respected that. Marketing's all about persuasion, anyway. Can you talk something up? Spin it? Find a new angle to pique interest? That's all it is—making bullshit look good. Just wrap it in a pretty bow."

He glances at me with a wink, and despite myself, I giggle and roll my eyes.

"Thanks for the pep talk," I say with a laugh, already trying to figure out how much of what he said I should take seriously.

The rest of the ride, he keeps asking me random questions, trying to keep the conversation alive. Every few minutes, he stretches his neck to flash a smile at me in the rearview mirror. He's actually kind of handsome. Older—at least forty—with a few gray hairs giving him a cool salt-and-pepper look. He reminds me of Ben Affleck if he'd never made it in acting. When we arrive, he hops out of the car and heads to the trunk to grab my bags.

"Be careful. It's a jungle out here," he says, handing them to me with a grin.

Then, he wishes me good luck, winks, and slides back into the driver's seat before driving off. Was he flirting with me or just being nice? I honestly don't know. It's something I've been struggling with these past few years, ever since high school. Back then, I was a painfully shy late bloomer with buck teeth, practically invisible to most men. Now, things are different. They notice me, they're helpful, friendly—even eager. But the ones who actually make a move? They're never the *ones* I'm interested in.

After graduating college, I'm finally moving out of my mother's house. I envisioned my life blooming after high school, but after a year on campus, it only deepened my disappointment. The cost of living on campus was more than I could afford. Despite working a part-time job as a hostess at Red Robin and receiving financial aid through FAFSA, I couldn't keep up. The debt piled up, forcing me to move back home with my mom.

I graduated with my bachelor's degree in marketing. And got accepted as an intern at Introspection, one of the biggest media companies in the world. My favorite professor, Mrs. Clark, had encouraged me to apply, promising to put in a good word for me. When the acceptance letter finally arrived in the mail two weeks ago, I was ecstatic. I had checked the mailbox every day for two months, it was the only thing I could think about; my ticket out.

When I got the news that Introspection would cover my room and board, I was ecstatic. I didn't have any money, and the thought of driving twenty-two hours to

New York City felt impossible. The three-hour flight they paid for was a gift—there was no point in bringing my car. It's New York City, after all. Who needs a car here? Everything about this feels like a dream, and I'm already in love with the city.

The apartment building they've placed me in is a literal skyscraper, the kind of luxury building you see in movies. Its massive windows wrap around the structure, reflecting the city lights like a crystal beacon. I can't believe I live here. Stepping inside, I'm blown away. Chandeliers hang like stars from the high ceilings, a beautiful fountain bubbles softly in the middle of the lobby, and Renaissance-style artwork lines the walls. I feel a mixture of excitement and discomfort, as though I don't quite belong here. Lost in thought, I accidentally bump into someone.

"Oh, I'm so sorry," I say, flustered.

The woman I've bumped into doesn't even acknowledge me. She strides past without a word, exuding confidence. She's tall, with rich auburn hair that glows in the light, streaked with highlights like the colors of a sunset. She's wearing burnt orange pleated slacks that fit her perfectly, paired with a cream cashmere sweater that hugs her slim, hourglass frame. The sound of her heels clicking against the marble floor echoes in my ears as she heads toward the restaurant next door. She's *fabulous*.

As I look around, I see stylish, beautiful people every-where—walking along the sidewalk outside the building and lounging in the lobby. I feel out of my depth. I head to the front desk, where the receptionist catches my eye. She's pretty, with minimal makeup and a polished appearance that suggests she might be around twenty-three. I can't help but wonder if she dreams of doing something else—maybe modeling. Her name tag reads *Ashley*. Fitting.

She looks up from her phone, her lips curling into a polite smile. "Hi, how can I help you?"

I introduce myself, hand over my ID, and she checks me in and hands me my key. I thank her as I head to the gleaming glass elevator. I get in and just as the doors are about to close, a woman hurries in, her heels clicking against the floor. She's looking down, a coy smile on her face, holding a martini glass that seems to have come straight from the bar. It's *her*. The fabulous woman I noticed earlier in the lobby—the one who bumped into me. Her natural red hair cascades over her shoulder and down to her tailbone, when she looks up, a little unsteady on her feet, some of her drink sloshes over the rim of her glass.

"Which floor?" she asks, her words slurred. She's drunk, but her playful tone catches me off guard.

At first, I didn't understand her, so we just stared at each other for a dull moment.

"Oh, uh, ten," I finally managed.

"Ah, me too," she replies, glancing back down at her phone.

The silence between us feels heavy, so I blurt out, "I'm Karma, by the way."

She looks up briefly, flashing a grin before returning her attention to her screen. When we reach our floor, she steps out without another word. I pull out my key and head down the hallway, searching for apartment 1021. She's walking in the same direction. She heads to apartment number 1016. As she struggles to unlock her door, she glances over her shoulder and catches me watching. She giggles, and I can't help but laugh too. A moment later, she stumbles into her room and shuts the door behind her with a loud slam. I finally find my room.

It's stunning. Immense windows flood the space with light, and it's already furnished: a suede La-Z-Boy couch, a wooden circular coffee table, a flat-screen TV, and a chic Renaissance painting that draws your attention. I let out a deep breath and take it all in.

The bedroom is enormous, featuring sleek black furniture—a vanity, a nightstand, and a queen-size bed dressed in a crisp white comforter and checkered, fashion pillows. On the nightstand, there's a bottle of champagne accompanied by a note that reads:

"Welcome, Karma, to Introspection Media. We hope you enjoy your stay and are elated to see you tomorrow. Love, your team."

2

Karma

IT'S 7 a.m. Last night, I barely slept, I spent hours trying to figure out what I'm going to wear. Ugh, I hate all my clothes. I thrift shop, because it's all I can afford. I throw on this charcoal blazer over a black bodysuit with black slacks. Slim and sexy look. Yeah, this will work. Oh, wait, does this make me look like a receptionist? Whatever, I'll look better once I do my makeup and hair.

As I approach the mirror, I notice two fresh pimples on my face. I pop them, they only bleed. Great. I press on them to stop the bleeding, but it doesn't help. With no time to waste, I dab concealer over the spots, though it barely hides them. I put on some mascara and a red-tinted lip gloss on my full lips, then pull my long, thick, dark brown curls into a high ponytail, pulling out a few pieces to frame my face. Staring at my reflection, I strike a pose, rehearsing how to introduce myself at work.

"Hi, I'm Karma. So thankful to be here, sir," I say

aloud, extending an imaginary handshake. I try again, adding some small talk. "Hi, I'm Karma. Where are you from? Oh, really? Ha-ha, I'm from Texas."

Wait, should I say I'm from Texas? Or should I be more specific? Maybe a big city, like Austin? No, Austin isn't *that* cool. What about Houston or Dallas? Dallas sounds good. It's not entirely a lie—Gruene is between the two, but no one knows where that is. Dallas it is.

I try again: "Hello, I'm Karma. I'm from Dallas. Where are you from?" That sounds awkward, too pushy. I need to relax. Smile more. Be outgoing but not overbearing. Speak when spoken to. Play it cool.

A notification dings on my phone, breaking my spiral. My Uber's out front. I take a deep breath, grab my bag, and head out the door. When the car pulls up to Introspection Media, I'm immediately overwhelmed.

The entrance is buzzing with people, all looking busy and important. They're walking briskly; coffees or phones in hand, radiating confidence. I feel so out of place. But I remind myself: fake it till you make it. I square my shoulders, lift my chin, and stride toward the entrance, trying to exude confidence.

Inside, I notice a woman with long brown hair and a radiant smile. She's greeting everyone and handing out what looks like itineraries. She's clearly older but has a youthful glow. Her outfit is so cute—white pencil skirt, a baby pink blazer, and a tucked-in white cotton shirt. Effortlessly chic. That's what I want to look like when I'm older.

She smiles warmly at everyone who passes, her energy is so welcoming.

I'm guessing she's one of our bosses, so I mustered the courage to introduce myself. Just as I open my mouth to speak, she suddenly calls out to someone behind me.

"Athena! Hi, gorgeous! So glad to see you!"

I turned to see the redhead from the elevator yesterday—*Athena*—as she strides over with her usual effortless grace. The woman I was about to address holds out her arms, and Athena does the same, the two embracing like old friends.

I glance down at the woman's name tag. *Kim Brown.* Wait—*Mrs. Brown.* That name rings a bell. She's the founder of the company. How does she know Athena?

Does Athena live in my apartment complex because she's an intern, too? If so, how do they already seem so close? What am I missing? As they hug and chat like long-lost friends, I'm left standing awkwardly by the doorway. Eventually, Athena excuses herself, saying she'd better get inside. Mrs. Brown hands me a flyer with a bright smile, and I take it, mumbling a thank-you as I trail behind Athena into the room. The place is stunning. It's like a lecture hall but far more luxurious with plush red velvet chairs, polished chestnut floors, and a grand stage at the front. A giant screen displays a slideshow about the company.

The room is already buzzing with energy; people chatting and laughing like old friends. I spot Athena seated a few rows ahead, rummaging through her purse.

Athena. Her name fits her perfectly. She's exactly what you'd imagine when you hear the name of a goddess. As I search for a seat. People are mingling, connecting so naturally. I envy how easy it seems for them. I glance around, trying to avoid making weird eye contact, but it keeps happening.

Then, a booming voice breaks through the chatter. "Everyone, find your seats!"

I freeze for a second, then quickly slip into the seat next to Athena. Maybe I can strike up a conversation—mention that we live in the same complex or something. The man at the front commands attention. He's tall, broad-shouldered, and bald, his artificial tan giving his skin an odd orange tint. His deep voice reverberates through the room as he begins.

"This is the beginning of your career—or, for some of you, the end. We are your alpha and omega. Over the next two months, you'll have to prove your worth through a series of tests and opportunities." The room goes silent. He pauses for effect, then continues, "Everyone! Look to the person on your right. Now look to the person on your left. *These are your competition.*"

I turn my head to the right and find myself looking at Athena. She barely glances my way before returning to her purse. I look away quickly, unsure of how to bridge the silence between us.

"Sorry if you came here to make friends," the man sneers. "The people here are your enemies. So, either be great, or at least be better than the person next to you.

Now find your sections and wait for instructions. Move!"

Everyone around me stands and begins walking with purpose, as if they know exactly where to go. Panic sets in. *Oh shit!* I realize why I have no idea what's happening. I missed orientation day because of a booking error, and now I'm completely lost. I decide to follow the crowd, hoping it leads me somewhere useful. We make our way down a sleek hallway and enter a room that screams "tech agency." Rows of cubicles and multi-screen computers fill the space, and someone explains that this will be our main workplace.

I scan the room, hoping to spot Athena. I'm hoping to be around at least someone remotely familiar. As I wander, trying not to look as lost as I feel, I feel a tap on my shoulder. Startled, I spin around and come face-to-face with a boy I had noticed earlier.

"Hey, you look a little lost. What section are you in?" he asks, his expression unreadable.

"Um, that's a brilliant question," I say, forcing a laugh. "I actually don't know. There was a problem with my flight, so I missed—" I notice just how handsome and unamused he looks.

"Yeah, I don't remember seeing you at the orientation," he cuts me off. "Go talk to Mr. Kelp. He'll tell you where you need to be."

Before I can respond, he turns and walks away without another word, leaving me standing there, feeling both embarrassed and frustrated. I glance around, hoping there's a receptionist or *anyone* else I can approach instead. But no, it has to be Mr. Kelp. I hesitate as I spot him through the glass walls of his modern, elegant office. The sleek design only adds to his intimidating presence. He's deep in conversation with someone, but even from here, I can feel his no-nonsense energy.

As I approach, he glances up briefly, raising his eyebrows in a way that makes me stop in my tracks. It's a look that says, *don't even think about interrupting me.* For a second, I feel like a deer caught in headlights, shrinking under his imposing presence. Why does he have to look at me like I'm some peasant daring to approach a king? If I hadn't missed my flight, I wouldn't be in this mess.

But here I am. I take a deep breath and force myself to take another step forward. Then someone grabs my arm. It's Athena, and she looks a lot happier to see me.

"Hey, Karma, right?"

I looked at her, puzzled. How does she know my name? Did she hear me that night and just ignore me?

Now seeing her up close I realized how pretty she is. She has piercing blue eyes. Medium-sized lips with a bigger bottom lip that gives her that natural pouty look. Long auburn hair with strawberry blonde highlights throughout and a perfect button nose.

"Your necklace, it says Karma and I feel like you look like your name." She laughs. "I remember seeing your name on the sign-in sheet and they called for you yesterday. But I didn't see you at orientation, and you are standing here like a lost puppy. So, I knew that had to be you! Come on! You're in my group!" She drags my arm. I'm so glad she found me.

As we sit down in our big cubicles and wait to be instructed, I look around. I love people-watching. It's one of my favorite things: studying others, trying to figure out what makes them tick, the way they do, and why they do the things they do. I'm great at reading people. Although Athena is a wildcard, in the short time I have known her, I have already seen three sides of her personality. As we wait, she talks to the boys next to her about what school they went to and what they plan to do afterward. They all seem so confident that they will remain here. One of them pans to me while I'm looking at my phone, opening and closing the same three apps, trying to appear as if I'm busy. He's the one who tapped me on the shoulder earlier.

He looks at me with his captivating light brown eyes and says, "Why weren't you here yesterday?"

He's cute. I blush as I explain to him how my flight got messed up, but before I can finish, the instructor walks in and begins speaking. She's a heavy, pale woman, well-spoken, wearing pleated pants and a flowy top.

"Good morning, everyone. Let's get started," she says, her tone brisk. "This internship will start with a major project—and, yes, it's a competition. You'll each be tasked with developing a pitch for the brand *Sunday's Best*—an iconic clothing brand from the 90s that has lost its momentum. Your goal is to propose a fresh, innovative way to revive the brand and boost their sales."

The room buzzes slightly with quiet murmurs, but the instructor quickly raises her voice to regain control.

"This will be individual work, not group work," she continues.

"At the end of the project, two interns will be sent home. The bureau hired too many interns and we have some logistical issues to resolve. So, the stakes are high."

The tension in the room thickens as her words sink in. My stomach flips. *Two people will be sent home.* The pressure is on, and I can feel the weight of it already.

We all pull out our laptops and start researching the company—its past advertisements, and the current state of its stocks, which are, unsurprisingly, quite low. As I scroll through the information, a memory pops into my head: *Sunday's Best*—the brand my mother used to wear all the time.

She'd go buy a new dress from them for every date with men she met at the bar or from pen pals she'd made while serving three years in jail for grand larceny.

My mother is infamous in our small town. She worked for a while as part of the cleaning crew on the set of the movie *Lover's Game*. She would sneak into the movie stars' trailers, stealing jewelry and clothing from some of the most famous people, while they filmed an adaptation of the popular sci-fi 80's book trilogy *Lovers Game*. My mother adored actors and dreamt of being an actress herself. She worked on that set for two years until she was caught. It made headlines in our tiny town, and for almost a year, the local newspaper ran a picture of her smiling mugshot under the headline: *"Single Mother Movie Set Employee Stole Over $100,000 Worth of Jewelry and Clothing."* The actual amount wasn't nearly that high, but it was quite a bit.

I was in middle school at the time, but my mom's stealing wasn't new. She had been doing it since I was a baby. I'd watch her go into stores with no money, then walk out with something—usually small, like a candy bar or lip balm. She always had a way of making it seem like it was no big deal. I remember once, she picked up an eyeliner and exclaimed, *"Five dollars for eyeliner? I'm not paying for that!"* before casually slipping it into her pocket. The movie set incident was the first time she was caught —and really reprimanded. My mom had a way of getting around trouble. She had the local police and security in her back pocket. All it took was a polite smile, a teary-eyed apology, and an outrageous sob story. One time, she told them she had cancer. Then that she'd just been robbed of everything she owned, or some other wild excuse. People believed her. She had a charm that was impossible to resist.

I've always admired my mom's beauty and her vivacious personality. She was magnetic—everyone loved being around her. Her laughter was infectious, and she had an energy that filled any room she entered.

When she went to jail, I had to live with my grandparents. They were the opposite of her—calm, poised, and entirely "normal." They had been married since they were nineteen, and their life together seemed so stable. I often wonder how my mom ended up so different from them. Maybe she was just bored with the calm, mundane, predictable life they led. She was an only child, and I'm sure she got whatever she wanted growing up. My grandfather had retired as an Air Force pilot, which meant he was often away, but my mom and grandma always had what they needed.

I asked my grandma why all this happened and she said Karma, your mother, had always been just different. She dropped out of school and moved out of the house when she was seventeen to live with her boyfriend, Richard - my father who was twenty-one at the time. Their relationship was full of turmoil—constant fighting, jealousy, breakups, and makeups.

Though, I never met my father. I've seen pictures of him from when they dated all those years ago. He had the look of a movie star. He is now married with three kids. I found this out when my mom went to jail. He reached out, apparently unaware I even existed. He said he did the math from the article about my mom's arrest, which included my age.

He called my grandma to confirm it, and that's when we spoke for the first time. We exchanged some awkward small talk—he even asked me about the weather. Before hanging up, he said he'd stay in touch, but he never did. Guess my mom was right when she said he was a nobody.

My mom told me he cheated on her. She found a number in his jeans one night when she did his laundry. The next day, she followed him after work, and watched him greet some skinny brunette woman with a kiss at a restaurant.

Heartbroken, she went back to his place, took his TV, laptop, watch, and gold chain; pawned them, and left with the money. She got a new job, a new phone number, and moved in with an old friend from high school in a town a few hours away. She never looked back. When my mom found out she was pregnant with me, she thought about answering my dad's calls—he had apparently been leaving her messages every day—but she wanted nothing to do with someone who didn't value her. By then, she had already moved on with a new boyfriend—her boss.

After our brainstorming session and running errands for coffee, we were let out for lunch. Mr. Kelp handed me a list of orders and told us to head to a place down the street called Everglore, a very bougie vegan restaurant. I had no idea what to order for myself, so I just asked the cashier what was the most popular thing and ordered it, and handed them the company credit card. My team of interns and I are in the digital marketing section, collaborating with the company's best. These are the people who can get the biggest stars to promote brands and have built strong relationships with top networks.

As we wait for our to-go orders, the four of us sit together at the table—me, Athena, and two guys. One of them is Brent, the guy who tapped me on the shoulder earlier, asking if I was lost. I overheard his name when his friend called after him. Brent is ridiculously handsome—caramel skin, a strong jawline, dark curly hair, full lips, and those light brown eyes that seem to glow. He looks like a racially ambiguous version of Brad Pitt.

My phone buzzes. It's Lucas again. I flip it face down on the table, ignoring it. I'm trying to leave all that drama behind, but I don't know how to tell him. Honestly, I don't even want to think about it anymore.

Brent and I lock eyes, and I quickly look away, only to find myself sneaking another glance. Oh my gosh, I need to stop staring. Finally, he breaks the silence.

"What's your name?" he asks.

My voice cracks as I answer, "Karma."

He chuckles, his gaze flicking from my face to my chest—at my necklace. I blush, feeling self-conscious.

"I thought you were just one of those spiritual girls," he teases.

I laugh. "No, not really. But my mom always says what you do will come back to you. You know, the whole universe's laws thing."

Everyone nods as if they've heard it before. Meanwhile, Athena is slouched over, glued to her phone, texting nonstop. She's the kind of person who leaves her ringer on just so everyone knows how many people are vying for her attention. Her fingers move quickly, her face set with focus.

Brent's friend suddenly returns to the table, carrying drinks in a tray and sporting a goofy grin. "Hey, bruv, I think the waitress wants me. She keeps giving me the eyes. Should I ask her out?" he said in a gritty voice.

Brent's friend Ryan is British, lanky with dirty blonde

wavy hair. His eyes are dark blue and his lips are thin. He's kind of cute, although nothing compared to Brent. Ryan is a harmless, nerdy type of guy. Brent looks behind him at the girl, shaking his head.

"Ryan, not every—oh, she is looking over here. Maybe you're right!"

"I say go for it," Athena says. "What do you have to lose?"

I see the waitress too, looking over, smiling, then she waves her hand. As to beckon him over.

"Oh, wow." I laugh.

Ryan looks at me with a sneer, raises his eyebrows, and stands up in a cocky manner over to the counter. We all watch as the girl behind the counter smiles at him, then turns back, grabs his wallet, and walks back. His smile drops after he thanks her, and walks back with his tail between his legs. We all laugh. Brent pats Ryan on the back and says,

"She had us all fooled, buddy."

"You should still have said something! You're a good-looking guy. She would probably say yes if you asked her out," Athena teases, smirking.

Ryan's dark blue eyes light up. He and Athena look at each other for a moment, he then looks at Brent. Then the staff call our names to tell us our food is ready. Brent steps forward, grabs the food and we start heading back.

Athena is walking with Ryan, ahead of us. I noticed that he kind of ran up alongside her to engage in conversation. Ryan doesn't really look like Athena's type. But I can tell Ryan is surely barking up that tree. She *did* throw him a bone.

I end up walking beside Brent. My palms start to sweat and my heartbeat increases. The last thing I wanted was to walk alongside him on the way back. I tried to strike up a conversation with Athena, but Ryan beat me to it. I offered to help carry the food, but Brent said he's got it. So now it's just us walking in an awkward silence. I pull out my phone. Maybe I should say something.

Ryan stops in his tracks, looks back at us and says, "Oh, bruv, I totally forgot the lemonade, I can't go back in there!" His face is kind of red with embarrassment. We all just look at each other.

"Karma and I will grab the lemonade. You guys go ahead so the food doesn't get cold. We'll catch up," Athena says, looping her arm through mine with a bright smile, like we're already best friends.

As we walk back toward the restaurant, her voice takes on a giddy, conspiratorial tone. "So, which one do you like?" she asks, sounding like a schoolgirl talking about crushes.

I laugh nervously. "What? I don't know. I don't really know them."

Athena tilts her head, narrowing her eyes slightly in playful annoyance. "Oh, come on. Which one do you think is cute? Brent, huh?" She smirks as her eyes lock with mine, and then bursts into laughter.

"I knew it!" she says, grinning. "He is hot, but he's not my type."

"What's your type?" I ask, genuinely curious. "Ryan?"

"No, umm... my type is rich and sexy. Yes, rich," she jokes, laughing at herself. "I don't know, though. I don't really have a type, you know? I just like what I like." She shrugs as we step up to the restaurant door.

An older man exits at the same time, catching sight of our smiles. He holds the door open for us, and we thank him quickly before rushing inside.

"But I thought you said Ryan was handsome?" I ask, raising an eyebrow.

Athena gives me a blank stare for a beat, then shrugs casually. "Yeah, I did, but that was mostly to get on his good side. We need to make friends here fast, and that's the best way. Haven't you heard? Everyone loves to hear the version of themselves that someone else fancies," she says, mimicking Ryan's accent with a playful English lilt.

"Ryan's, all right though not bad looking, but that waitress is way out of his league. I don't know what he was thinking,"

I giggle. We are now next in line. She orders the lemonade and an avocado egg sandwich as we wait for our order. Athena looks at my shoes and then up at me.

Her face lights up and says, "Oh my gosh, where did you get those shoes? They're so cute!"

I look down at my shoes. They are Boston Birkenstocks. I thought they looked cute and casual for the first day. "Thanks! I got these for Christmas last year. My grandpa got them for me, who knew he had taste."

"I love them. They go great with your cardigan that oh that color even brings out your eyes, you really have pretty eyes."

I'm blushing. "Wow, thank you, that's so nice!"

Then Athena just looks at me with this goofy smile. "See, you literally just ate that shit up."

My smile falters, confused for a moment, before I realize what we were just talking about.

I pause and say, "Oh, okay. Well, I think compliments have more of an impact when they come from someone really beautiful."

Athena, distracted by a notification on her phone, looks up and narrows her eyes at me. "Ahhh, you bitch."

I laugh just as her name is called for the order. As we head back, we chat about being single and bond over how much of a dick we think Mr. Kelp, the boss, is. We mimic his pompous tone and exaggerated mannerisms, giggling the whole way.

When we get back with the drinks, the scene has already shifted. Everyone is at their desks, eating while working on their laptops. They're talking and laughing about something from the bar last weekend. One girl is blushing furiously, clearly embarrassed by whatever story they're teasing her about. I wonder what happened that night.

My phone dings. It's *him* again.

As I move to sit down, one of the guys—he's the head

of digital marketing—looks over at me and says, "No, get up. Don't eat here with us. Go home. You're all done for the day."

I glance toward where I thought Athena was standing, but she's already gone. "Oh. Okay," I mumble, grabbing my things. "All right, thanks. See you guys tomorrow."

No one acknowledges me, and I head for the door. The other interns are already gone. Maybe I'll catch up with Athena later. Walking out the back, I spot a big black truck parked in the farthest corner of the lot. One of the back doors is open, and someone is reaching for something inside. The door clicks shut behind me, and I instinctively glance toward the truck. Our eyes meet. It's Brent. I quickly turn my head and start walking toward Main Street. I need to get out of this parking lot.

After a few steps, I glance back. Brent's truck hasn't moved. Feeling uneasy, I pick up my pace, determined to get out of his line of sight. I need to find a coffee shop, somewhere to sit and regroup. I pull out my phone to check for the nearest one, but my connection is terrible. Frustrated, I shove it back into my pocket and decide to follow the flow of people heading toward the street.

New Yorkers always seem to know exactly where they're going—especially when it comes to finding coffee. I figure I might as well follow their lead. I need to get familiar with the city anyway. Maybe this is how people become locals—stumbling across cool niche spots, meeting new people, and carving out their own little corner of the city.

I tell myself I'm putting myself out there, letting things flow, just going with it. Like Athena, she seems fun, easygoing, and effortlessly magnetic. The boys clearly like her, and I have no doubt she could help me navigate this new world in New York City. The thought makes me roll my eyes at myself. Geez, I wish I *was* her. She's so naturally beautiful with her long red hair, her perfect little nose, those full pouty lips, and light blue eyes. But it's not just her looks—it's her energy. Her aura. People are just *drawn* to her. She's so charismatic, so vibrant, that it feels impossible not to enjoy being around her.

I wandered into this small indie-looking coffee shop. Entering, I scanned the shop, my eyes catching the Bob Marley posters. Beads adorned the walkways, while soothing R&B music filled the air.

Surfing the menu, I'm thinking about getting a medium coffee with oat milk, then I have a sudden urge to pee. I'm not sure where the bathrooms are. I don't see any signs and workers are busy taking orders. So, I just walk into one door in the back. The hallway here is narrow and has light blue walls with crackled paint. With a mop and a bucket in the corner. There are only three doors, one of them to the right says, 'Employees only', and the other door is at the end of the dark hallway. So, I go to the first door on my left.

I push it open, and immediately, the darkness makes me hesitate. I can barely make out two figures moving in the room. One is leaning on a desk, and the soft sounds of moaning fill the air. I squint, confused, trying to make sense of what I'm seeing. As my eyes adjust to the dark, I realize this isn't a bathroom at all—it's an office. And the two figures are men—one on his knees, the other leaning against the desk with his head thrown back.

Frozen, I stare for a moment longer, the realization sinking in. Then, in a burst of panic, I scream, "Oh, sorry!" and bolt out of the room.

I can't believe what I just saw. More importantly, I can't believe who I just saw.

3

Diary entry- 5 years ago

MY MOTHER HASN'T BEEN the same since my sister disappeared. She takes all her anger out on me. She has also been drinking more and not sleeping so she could *watch me*. Whatever that's supposed to mean. We fight all the time now. Like big fights yelling and screaming across the house. She even slapped me in front of the sheriff.

Apparently, that was the last straw, after us fighting, and me missing school for a month. CPS got involved even though I'm practically an adult. I can take care of myself. They told me I'd either have to go into foster care or move in with my dad, who, according to my mom, is an evil drug lord that I haven't seen since I was three years old. I chose to live with him. Wow, I'm kind of like Dani now, an orphan.

I met my dad at the airport. I remember little about

him. Besides that, he always had gel in his hair and smelled of cologne. And the nicknames he had for us as kids, Bunny for me and Rabbit for my sister because she was older.

When I see my dad waiting for me with a welcome home banner, it warms my heart. At least he is happy to see me. Living with my dad differs from my mom, but they have many similarities. They're both not home often. So, I still spend a lot of time alone, especially since I'm in online school now. My dad said I would have to do online school because we might have to move around frequently.

My mother told a few stories about my father, mostly negative ones. She told me about how they met in Vegas. She was there for her best friend's bachelorette party. At a hotel called the Caesar's Palace. Which has a huge casino inside and he was playing craps, and he called her over from far away saying.

"Excuse me, beautiful, in the blue dress." My mom looked down, forgetting what color she was wearing. Her friends egged her on to go join him, saying he was cute and looked wealthy.

He asked her to be his lucky charm and to blow on the dice for him. She did. That night he won fifteen dollars and the next day she canceled her flight back home. She stayed with him, went shopping, ate at all these fancy restaurants, and stayed at the best hotels. Later, she noticed the money was running out. And how she never saw him go to work, let alone know what he did for work.

When she asked, my dad told her, "I make money, that's what I do for work." He would then quickly change the subject.

My mom later would find things like trick dice in his laundry and burner phones in his drawers. After she found out she was pregnant she thought she'd be better off ignoring it. Then the next day my dad showed up with another twenty thousand dollars.

When she asked him where it came from, he said it came from a trust fund. That he didn't tell her because he didn't want her to have a skewed view of him because he came from money. She had my sister, then quickly became pregnant with me, then my dad proposed.

My mom kept asking when they were getting married and he'd say, "Oh, in a year when I receive my full trust" and then a year would pass and it'd be another excuse.

Then my mom threatened she would take us and leave him if they didn't get married, so they went to the courthouse. That's how they found out my father had a warrant for his arrest in a few states. The authorities quickly arrested my dad for fraud. That was the last time my mom allowed us to see him.

Mostly, she just told us awful stories about him apparently being a drug lord. I don't know if it is true or not. My mother does have a reputation of being dramatic and stretching the truth. She barely knows what's going on now, between all the pills and wine.

Hanging out with my dad has been interesting. I found out we have a lot in common. We like the same food, TV shows. I got him to watch reality TV, and he's obsessed with it now. But it's getting a little weird because my dad and I live in a hotel. He said it was only temporary but it's been a month already.

4

Karma

ONE OF THE great things about New York is how easy it is to disappear into the crowd. No one notices you; no one cares. It's a relief, really, it's the polar opposite of the south as I make my way to the subway. Two stops later, I'm back on my street, but my mind is racing.

I can't stop replaying what I just saw at the coffee shop. Isn't he married? To a woman, no less? And he's my *boss.* What if he fires me before I even really get started?

He could be making that call right now. What am I going to do? By the time I get back to my apartment, I'm pacing around my room, too anxious to even think about my project. The worst part? I completely forgot to grab a coffee in the middle of all this mess.

Why did this have to happen to me? Maybe I should just pretend it didn't. Act like I didn't know it was Mr. Kelp. I mean, I've only met him once—it's totally plausible I wouldn't recognize him in just a couple of seconds, right? And anyway, he probably won't even recognize *me*. He doesn't even know my name... does he?

I suck in a breath, trying to calm myself, but it's no use. I can't get the look on his face out of my mind. It was like he *did* recognize me. Or maybe I'm imagining it. God, I hope I'm imagining it. And then there's his wife. Does *she* know?

Does she have *any* idea what's going on? I wonder what she's like. I've only heard whispers about her—people speak of her like she's some kind of mythical creature. The chair of Introspection. I've heard she's ruthless, that she's made employees cry.

Curiosity takes over, and I sit down at my laptop to look her up. *Kathy Kelp.* A quick search pulls up Google images, and there she is. She looks young, maybe thirty or thirty-five. Tall and thin, with bronze skin, dark brown upturned eyes, rosy lips, and a sharp, square jaw. Her hair is a sleek, straight bob—very corporate chic. I found a picture of her with the president of Introspection, smiling for a press photo when she was promoted.

Next, I searched for her name on Facebook. To my surprise, she has a public profile. A little thrill runs through me as I click on it. But there's hardly anything there. I can't tell if she's just not active or if there's more content hidden because we're not friends. Either way, it leaves me feeling... unsettled.

Her profile picture shows her smiling in a tailored pantsuit, the quintessential "take me seriously" look. The background is predictable—a photo of her standing on top of a mountain, arms spread wide, as if she'd just conquered the hike. She looks athletic, the kind of person who probably played a sport in college. Scrolling further, I see she attended Berkeley and graduated ten years ago —the same year she got married. That's all I can really gather.

There's a link to her husband's profile, *Mark Kelp*. Curious, I clicked on his profile. His page is nearly empty, with just a simple profile picture of him smiling. No cover photo. "No posts yet," his profile reads. Disappointing. I go back to her profile, double-checking that I'm signed in to the right account. I even triple-check, just to be sure.

After a moment of hesitation, I sent her a friend request—just in case I might need access later. Satisfied, I log out, close all the tabs, and take a deep breath. I head to the shower, trying to wash the tension of the day away. Once I'm clean and in bed, I turn on my comfort show, and let it lull me into a restless sleep.

5

Diary entry- 5 years ago

I FOUND out what my dad does. To my surprise, Mom was right, kind of. I'm still not entirely sure. I just know that his name is definitely not John C. Quinn or Mary Kay Bishop like the names on these credit cards. His name is Zeus Drakos. He has checkbooks in so many people's names, none of which are his, and all this mail says he's applied for or has been denied credit cards in names far removed from his own.

I wasn't snooping; I was just bored. My dad enrolled me in an online school. It has been exhausting but still only takes up about five hours out of the day and the rest is mine to do what I please. I just wanted to know more about my dad in this kind of suite of a hotel room we have. He has a lot of stuff here for someone who moves a lot for work, which in this case I guess is scamming. I asked my dad what he did for work once I saw how nice the hotel was.

My dad said he works with numbers in his thick Cuban accent. Which he turns on and off depending on the company we have. I asked him, "Is it like insurance or an accountant?"

"Both," he said. I giggle as if he was making a joke, but it seems like he was serious. He was gone most of the day, starting at 6 am. He's an early bird, something I have not inherited. So, every day I wake up. He's not here, he comes back in the evenings. In a suit, always a suit. What con man wears a suit? I'm going to find out more. His MacBook is on his bed, *his perfectly made bed,* I notice. His laptop has a lock. I tried a few things. My name didn't work, nor did my sister's, nothing. Giving up on the laptop, I keep going through his drawers. I found more letters about loans and credit cards for ten to fifty thousand dollars.

Then I go into the closet. There is a shoebox filled with different IDs/driver's licenses for different states and passports. Does he make fake IDs too? Stunned, I sat there on the floor. Despite never knowing my dad, I never expected him to be like this. It's unbelievable that my mom was right. I hear him walk in. I try to put everything up as fast as I can, but he finds me. We both just look at each other. I can see the anger on his face, then the acceptance.

He then says to me in a calm voice, "So what have you learned?"

Pointing to the things scattered across the floor, "Why —did you lie to me?" I ask, my voice breaking.

"I said I work with numbers, and I do, as you can see," he said.

"Why?" *I can't believe my mom was right.* I just sat with my disappointment and acute fear.

"You never win by playing fair, darling; you know that."

6

Karma

I WAS SO anxious I barely slept last night. The only thing on my mind was finishing my project for Sunday's Best Clothing. The revamp is due today, but my presentation feels more like a high school art project than something professional. It seemed like a creative idea at first, but now it just feels juvenile. The presentations start at 7:30, so I need to be there by 7. It's too late to make any changes now.

It's 6:30 a.m., and I'm dressed in dark-wash, straight-leg Levi's that make my butt look good, a fitted black long-sleeve shirt, and small black kitten heels. I can't decide if I look like a substitute teacher or an over-eager 18-year-old going to her first interview. I'm curious what Athena will wear.

As I'm gathering my things, there's a knock at the door. I freeze. Who would be knocking this early? My mind immediately jumps to Mr. Kelp. Did he find out where I live? Introspection is paying for this place, so it wouldn't be hard for him to figure it out. What if he's here to confront me about yesterday? My heart starts racing. Mr. Kelp is a big guy. If he's angry... I hear another bang on the door, louder this time. Panicked, I look around for a weapon and grab the nearest thing—a lamp. It's not much, but it's better than nothing. I tiptoe to the door, gripping the lamp tightly, and then I hear a woman's voice.

"Hello? Karma?"

I pause. Is it Kathy Kelp? My stomach drops.

"Karma, open up! It's Athena! Hurry! Are you sleeping?"

Relief washes over me as I put the lamp down to my waist and open the door, annoyed but grateful.

"Hey, Athena. It's a little early," I say, trying to hide my irritation.

She huffs, brushes past me, and plops onto my bed like she's been here a million times. "Woah, what's with the lamp? Were you gonna try to *kill* me?" she says in a melodramatic voice, hand to her chest and a fake shocked expression.

I giggle nervously.

"Well, I didn't know who was banging on my door at 6 a.m."

She rolls her eyes.

"I got ready super-fast and was bored, so I came to

hang out. Oh, and I ordered us a car. No need to take the train and walk this morning."

That's Athena—always breezing in uninvited but somehow managing to make herself welcome.

"Oh, okay, thanks, where's your project"

Athena looks at me confused

"In my email?" She says, looking down at my desk, "Did you make a poster board? What is this high school?" She just looks at me blankly, then laughs.

"Yeah."

"Girl what the hell, um actually no. I think it's cute 3D visuals. It'll make you stand out!" she says while she tries to hold in her laughter.

I blush in embarrassment.

"Yes, I wanted to do something different. Because I know everyone will come with a PowerPoint," I lie. "I want to stay, to be memorable".

"Our car is downstairs. Come on!" Athena says as she jumps off the bed.

I love that her outfit is so chic and expensive looking. With her high waisted palazzo pants perfectly tailored, and her silk baby pink fitted button-up that shows off her collar bones. I wonder if she'd ever let me borrow that top?

"I like your outfit," I yell as I speed walk behind her. She walks so fast.

"Thanks. I bought it from a cute boutique in Manhattan. You should come with me next time I go shopping. I need some more work clothes. My regular day-to-day clothes are a little too... ummm."

"Casual?" I say.

"No slutty."

We laugh. Once we make it downstairs, we walk toward the car. The man driving sees us and jumps out to open the door for Athena and I.

"For Whitney?" he asks

"No—" I say.

Athena interrupts, "Yes, sorry to Introspection please."

I just looked at her puzzled. She doesn't acknowledge my confused glare.

She just smiles as she checks her phone and says to me, "Are you nervous?"

I shrug, shake my head slightly as I look at her inquisitively. I still can't figure her out, I have never met someone as enigmatic as herself.

"Mr. Kelp seems like such a hard ass I wonder who's going to lose?" she says.

"Ryan," I say.

"No, Americans love British people too much. His accent just makes him seem more articulate and interesting. What a fucking prick, huh?" she says.

"No, you are right. What if that's his angle? Imagine, what if his accent is fake? We have to quiz him to see if he's actually English, like make him answer One Direction and Ed Sheeran trivia questions, right?" I say.

Athena gasps. "Yes, you're a genius! If he gets three or more wrong, we have to call the cops and get him fired."

"One thousand percent," I say, we both let out a little giggle. We get to Introspection a little early, so we decide to get a coffee.

While we're walking there, I see Brent's car in the same spot in the back of the Introspection building. I wonder why he got here early as well. Maybe it's because he's just as nervous as us. I'm super anxious not just because of the presentation, but if Mr. Kelp recognized me from the other night. I don't know what I'd even say.

As I walk into Introspection, I don't see any of the bosses. It is just us interns. Brent and I make eye contact and butterflies flutter around my stomach. I'm not sure if I'm just staring at him, and he can feel me doing that. Or if he's looking at me as much as I look at him? I don't know. I hope he doesn't think I stare at him. I need to stop looking at him. He probably thinks I'm weird now.

I follow Athena hoping she is going to sit at an empty table. Instead, she looks back at me, and smiles as she struts over toward the table with the boys. Brent was laughing at Ryan as we sat down. Athena looks at Brent and asks what is so funny as she plops down in her seat.

"Nothing much, just this idiot forgot his flash drive at home," Brent says.

Ryan groans, rolling his eyes.

"I literally put it on the counter next to my phone so I won't forget it after I got out of the restroom, I don't know how I forgot it."

I look at him laughing. Ryan laughs as well, shaking his head. Now that I'm really looking at him, there is something appealing about him—like a charming guy you'd sit next to in study hall. He has a pleasant smile and is easy to be around; husband material.

Meanwhile Brent's deep in conversation with Athena about his project, and I feel a twinge of jealousy. He is wearing a nice, fitted navy blue sweater with the sleeves rolled up, showing off his muscled forearms and big sexy hands. The rest of his outfit is all black, making him look effortlessly polished. He looks so good. His clear caramel skin glows effortlessly, as his beautiful smile lights up his face while his thick eyebrows frame his face. I look around, seeing that Mr. Kelp is here. My heart is beating so fast. Mr. Kelp doesn't make eye contact with me. Maybe he didn't recognize me. Hopefully.

I look over at Ryan and he's looking more nervous by the minute.

"Do you think it's better if they think I just woke up late, right?" Ryan says, his voice laced with both hope and uncertainty

"Mr. Kelp is here already." Brent announces glancing toward the door. Across the table Ryan grins wryly.

"Or better if I had explosive diarrhea and excused myself, which I kind of feel coming on?" He adds, his eyes darting around as if checking for an escape route.

Athena scrunches her face, the corners of her mouth twitching in a mix of amusement and disgust "Eww," she murmurs

Ryan leans back shrugging in a way that mixes apology and with a touch of exasperation

"Sorry I get nervous shites," he says, running a hand through his hair as he shifts his weight from one foot to the other.

Athena chuckles softly and shakes her head, her eyes crinkling with genuine amusement as she reaches for her phone.

Ryan glances around. "We're early, anyway. I'm going home to get my flash drive. If they call my name, just make up something, I don't care," he declares. Without waiting for a response, he pushes himself up, dropping his chair with a soft thud, and dashes out the door.

I watch him leave, my eyes following his retreating figure until he disappears down the hall. At that moment Athena's phone rings. She stands up immediately and strides towards the exit, her heels clicking briskly on the tile floor.

Left alone with Brent at the table, an awkward silence settles between us. I fidget with the edge of my poster, my gaze flickering between him and everyone else walking in and out. I don't know what to say. Maybe I should ask him where he's from or—

"Hey, what's your angle on the project?" Brent asks, breaking the quiet, offering a small smile leaning forward.

I stutter for a moment "Umm, I um, well, just," I trail off gesturing toward my poster.

Brent glances at the poster and then back at me,

raising an eyebrow, "Oh, wow, you did a poster. That's old school of you." His voice is soft and eyes are attentive.

I feel my face grow red. "Um, yeah, I guess I didn't know if we'd have access to the projector. And I don't think it would give the same vision if I did it on the computer," I say as I point out all the magazine cut-outs, I used to get my point across.

"By centering pop culture around the brand. Being inspired by the new generation and what they want, not what they already have and know. And putting their idols in it. New and shiny, not borrowed or used as an adaptation." I say.

I look up at Brent, catching his beautiful light brown eyes, nodding his head, looking acutely impressed. I feel heat rush through my entire body. I now notice how close we are. I know we weren't this close to begin with. Has he leaned closer to me? It doesn't matter how we got close. I just know I like it. Then I asked him what his angle was. He runs his hand through his dark loose curly hair.

"It's top secret." I roll my eyes then he says, "Oh, come on, how else am I supposed to keep you on your toes?" His voice, deep and smooth.

I giggle. I was going to ask him where he was from. He has an accent that sounds East Coast, maybe he's a local. Before I get to ask him, Athena comes back.

She smiles and says, "Oh, my gosh, Ryan is not even back yet!" She laughs, looks at me with her phone out. "What do you think about these shoes? I was thinking about buying these for when we go out this weekend."

I glance at her phone. The shoes are some vintage cheetah print high heels. What really catches my eye is the price of fifteen hundred dollars. *I wonder how she has all this money and fancy clothes?*

"Oh, we're going out?" I say.

"Yeah of course, what else are we supposed to do? It is basically homework. We need to go out and meet people, you know marketing. Right?" She turns to Brent.

"You're coming too, right?"

"Probably not. I have to work," Brent says, and then Kathy Kelp comes and announces that something came up and presentation time will be pushed back.

"So go grab a coffee, take a piss, whatever you need I'll be back shortly. Plan to be back in thirty-five minutes or such," she says, shoots us a forced smile then speed walks to her office. I wonder what's that about, maybe she found out about what I saw yesterday. My heart starts to race.

Brent looks over at me shaking his head. "Ryan, that boy has always had equally the best and worst luck. I have never understood it, like this one time he peed his pants from laughing too hard on a baseball trip. Then at that same time the bus stopped for gas and he was able to change, clean up and buy some new shorts" he chuckles.

I laugh when he gets up and says he's going to grab a coffee; he even asks me if I want one. I politely say no, if I have a coffee I will poop my pants. I'm way too anxious right now, with Mr. Kelp, my presentation, and Brent. My stomach is doing flips already. A couple of other people walk out as well as Athena. So, I'm left here alone. I just pull out my phone and I see a notification from Lucas pop up again. I click on his profile and marvel at his photos.

He's always been so good-looking. With his athletic body, curly blonde hair and green eyes. He keeps saying he loves me but I know he wouldn't if he found out who I really am, and what I did. My heart wrenches a little thinking about it. I close out of that and click on this video compilation called *'Cats Being Perfect'*. I watch those for about fifteen minutes then everyone starts to trail back in.

Ryan comes back panting. "Hey, they haven't started yet, have they?"

"No, you made it in just enough time." Now the room is full, and one of the employees has dimmed the light to show the PowerPoint screen. One of the managers started to call names, to start the presentations on how to revamp the Sunday's Best Clothing brand. The first girl to go did really well, very eloquently spoken.

I don't see Mr. Kelp around, making me feel better. His wife is still here in the corner; she looks just like her photos. Maybe even better. Everyone does pretty well, Athena kills it, and even gets a few laughs. Ryan does well even though you can see his sweat stains from fifteen feet away. Then it's Brent's turn, he looks good up there, standing at six feet, with a strong build; so confident and sexy. I have to figure out his last name so I can look him up online later. I can't help but wonder if he has a girlfriend. What's he like in bed? What kind of girl he likes, and how he sounds when he moans.

My daydreaming is cut short when I hear the words I have been rehearsing for the last eight hours. Is he fucking stealing my idea? He had his idea and now he's riffing off basically what I told him. Just changing a few words. What the hell? I'm going to look like an idiot and like I'm copying him. After he's done, everyone claps. My jaw is left open.

Athena looks at me, taps my jaw and says, "Babe, you're drooling."

"No, I Uh, He stole my—" Then I hear my name get called. Great. I go up there with my board and tail in between my legs. I introduce myself and I just start pointing at my board and saying things that come to my head. I try to improvise by remixing what I'd rehearsed. I know I sounded like an idiot, I kept saying "um" and "like" over and over.

When I finally said, "Yeah that's it." In the end, everyone clapped. I felt so stupid and embarrassed I don't even remember what I said. "How bad was that?"

She shakes her head. "It wasn't that bad. You're fine. But a girl with the stutter? That's horrible. As long as you're better than the last person, you're golden."

I look toward Brent as he is talking to Ryan. He hasn't even looked at me once since he finished his presentation. My heart sinks further. What if I get fired from this? They probably think I copied him and that I'm not a good presenter? Or that I'm stupid and lazy. Because I didn't write my speech and I brought a *stupid* poster board.

My heart hammered in my chest as a cold creeping chill slides down my spine. My palms grow slick with sweat. I need to do something—I have to do something. I did not come this far to just get turned around. I need to find Mr. Kelp.

7

Diary entry- 5 years ago

MONEY IS RUNNING OUT. My dad hasn't told me, but I have just noticed that we don't go to fancy restaurants anymore. There was also a note on the door about a late payment notice. We had McDonalds for dinner last night. And he seems on edge. He hasn't given me an answer about teaching me whatever he does, I mean I have no clue. But I want to help. I just know I don't want to end up like my mother, a wino with a pill problem stuck in our hometown.

But today at noon he tells me to get dressed, we go have lunch downstairs in our resort-like hotel. Then he puts our meal on a random room number. I asked him why he did that; he said that I must have *misheard* him. This must mean all the money is gone. I tell him I can help. Now I can see by the look on his face that he's really considering it.

He agrees begrudgingly. "One thing you can do is

cash out this debit card." He gives me these shades and does my hair to mimic the ladies in her driver's license photo. My dad tells me this is a rich kid's card. They'd never notice. Her name is Valerie Bowman.

My father explains to me one way he gets money and people's sensitive information. He gives front desk girls at high end restaurants and hotels petition forms for 'save the children', 'higher state minimum wage', 'better education', where they put their first and last name, email, birthday (to make sure they are over 18) and address. He takes those forms and emails them about their cards being charged thousands of dollars. And that they need to verify their information, or that their social security number got leaked, and they need to follow this link to dispute charges. If they don't respond to the emails, my dad makes fake IRS letters with the link to his website, which we only access by using VPNs.

He makes me study Valerie Bowman's information, her social security number, birthday, mother's maiden name, and the town she was born in. He quizzes me on the way there. Once we got to the bank, I walked up to the bank teller and tell her my request for five thousand dollars. She makes me verify some information. Then she goes to the back for about ten minutes, making me a little nervous. The bank teller comes back with a smile on her face and an envelope with all the money. My hands are sweating as I grab the money. I tell the lady thank you and speed walk out of there. My God that was so thrilling! I did it!

This is so easy. We do that for a couple of days to get by. Buying wigs for the other identities, going shopping and eating at the best restaurants until one day. We get ambushed by three big guys that make us get into this sprinter. They then escort us to this hotel that has a lower-level basement where this office is. They tell us to sit in front of this older, heavy white guy behind the desk with a cigar in his mouth. It smells like lavender and tobacco in here.

You couldn't imagine a crooked CEO who doesn't look like him. With his Rolex, black hair slicked back, wearing a suit, he smiles and claps as we arrived.

"I'm happy you can make it!" in a nefarious tone. He tells my father that he owes him money. My dad says he will give it to him and that he's started another. And the man cuts him off.

"I know you're gonna give me my money, but I'm bored and I'm tired of waiting. I'm going to need some collateral. You know?" He says as his eyes trace my body.

"Like that," he points to me as if I'm an object. "That's perfect," he says.

"What? No, I'll have the money."

"No, I think I want her. My mind is made up. And who is this? I've never seen you with a woman as long as I've fucking known you. You've been holding out on me? She's better looking than most of these hookers here, where did you find her?"

My dad doesn't answer, he just has this look of defeat on his face.

"Eh, never mind doesn't matter." He looks at one guy that brought us in. "Take her up to my bedroom and get rid of him." I can't believe this is happening.

I look at my dad and he has a blank stare directly to the floor. Then glances me with a fake toothy smile and takes my hand and whispers through his teeth. "Everything is going to be okay, don't be scared I'll get you out of there. Just stall and buy yourself some time, okay? You're strong, you can't act scared even if you are. Smile, okay?"

"Yeah, say your sweet goodbyes you won't see him again, baby," My dad gets taken away.

He looks back at me and smiles. Following his instructions, we head up to the hotel. I try to make conversation and act calm, like I'm not being sex trafficked. I forget most of what we talked about. I might have blacked out. Suddenly I just replay in my head what my dad said, "Don't act scared, smile." *Smile and buy time, dad is coming.* I feel like I'm running out of time now, because I'm in the room by myself on the bed, while the man is in the shower.

The two big guys are standing outside the door, making sure I don't run away. I wonder where they took my dad? I panic; I need to do something. I look around for weapons. Nothing but maybe a lamp? I try to lift it up, but it's glued to the table. That won't work. I hear the shower stop and my heart sinks.

He takes a few minutes to get out. He steps out of the bathroom in a long white hotel robe. With his towel in his hand drying the rest of his hair, he smiles when he sees me. I make myself smile back as I sit on the edge of the bed. I stare at the red carpet, stained from dark liquor and cigars. I can smell it, this room reeks of stale whiskey, musk and cigarettes. The TV is on in the corner. It's the news they are talking about how the water supply has become toxic in Chicago. I'd do anything to be there right now. He walks toward me.

"How long have you been doing this?" he says. Does he think I'm a prostitute? I need to play along.

"Um, not long." He is now standing over me.

"I can tell." His lips twisted into a sinister smile. "I like that though." He caresses my chin. I'm disgusted. "I don't like all those nasty, used up, stretched out whores." He chuckled.

I don't think my dad's coming anymore. What if they killed him? I feel my eyes water. I pop up.

"I have to go to the bathroom," I blurt, my voice fragile and shaking.

He grabs my arm, tightly stopping me from moving. "Do not try anything, slick bitch. If you're not back in two minutes, I'll come to drag you by your hair, you understand?" he said with a cold edge in his voice.

"Yes, I just have to pee," I say.

"Well, hurry the fuck up. I'm not gonna be waiting all day."

I walk into the bathroom and I see my reflection. I cry. This is it for me. I look for windows but there is no latch to open them. I'm guessing it's because we are on the 6th floor. He took my phone, so I don't know what I'm going to do right now.

If I have sex with him, I could wait till he falls asleep and sneak out. Or I could try to make a run for it but I won't get far between me and three men. I'm shaking. I look in the mirror and tell myself I only need to survive this night, and I will find a way out later.

There are maids and other guests here. I'll be able to get out. Wiping my tears. I walk out, trying not to make eye contact. Feeling utterly depleted that my dad's still not here.

Now, I know he's not coming. I walk back out to the bedroom. He smiles, stands up and tells me to sit on the bed. I do as he says, he takes off his robe and reveals himself standing in front of me with his hairy, old, pudgy body. I start to cry again; he slaps me and grabs my jaw with his gnarled hands. Then I hear a bang on the door.

"I'm busy!" he yells, then another bang comes at the door. Then the sound of a struggle.

I hear three gunshots go off. Then a kick at the door, then another until the door breaks off. It's my dad, his face is almost unrecognizable with all the blood covering it and the crazed look on his face. He enters, holding a pistol up with one hand at the nude man in front of me, without a second thought shoots the man three times; first in the head, then two in the chest.

The gunshots are so loud they make my ears ring. I hold my hands over my ears and crouch my head down. My dad grabs me by the arm and runs out of the room, toward the emergency exit. In the hall, I hear people screaming and running the opposite way. We run to this random beat-up red Toyota pickup that has the emergency lights on.

He yells at me, "Get in!" Then we speed off.

"What's going on?" I say, still crying.

"We're leaving! That's what we're doing, okay? We're okay now. Everything's okay," he says with a forced, pleading smile.

Which is horrifying, being that he still has blood all over him. I look down at my clothes, so do I. We drive for like five hours until we're in a town an hour away from Atlanta.

My dad tries to clean his face off with his button-up shirt. It's not working well, so he makes me check into the hotel with the cash. The hotel is blue and one story, with all the rooms having outside doors. It looks more like a motel 6.

Once I enter, the hotel clerks shoot me a concerned look. I laugh and tell them I spilled cranberry juice all over me, trying to drink it on the highway. They nod and smile politely; give me my key and tell me my room number is 710. I go back to my dad's car and help him with the suitcases.

Once we get in the room, he throws his flip phone down the toilet and takes a shower. We don't talk about anything that happened. The only thing we speak about is what we are getting for dinner. It's 11:30 pm. Not much is open right now. So, we order Chinese takeout and watch TV till we fall asleep.

8

Karma

AFTER THE PRESENTATIONS ARE OVER, I feel like I want to die. I absolutely hated my presentation. My voice was shaky, my entire plan fell apart, all because of Brent. I can't stand him—what a sly little rat. I thought we were flirting, that there was some chemistry there. I thought he liked me, but now I wonder if that was his angle all along. It's pathetic, really. I'm shaking with anger just thinking about it.

Kathy Kelp is speaking now, going on about how everyone did well and how we'll find out the final decision on Monday. But I can't even focus. I'm so furious, and I need to talk to Mr. Kelp in private. The moment they dismiss us for lunch, I don't engage with anyone—I just bolt straight to the bathroom for a quick pep talk. I have to gather my thoughts before I confront him.

Once I'm ready, I head straight to Mr. Kelp's office. I barge in without knocking. "I need to speak with you!"

He and another manager, Mr. Ward, are in there. Mr. Ward turns to me with a frown, clearly annoyed. "Excuse me? It can wait. As you can see, we're busy talking." says Mr. Ward.

I lock eyes with Mr. Ward, trying to stay firm. "No, if you don't mind, Ward, we'll revisit this sometime this week."

Mr. Ward looks at Mr. Kelp then me, confused, then chuckles.

"Fine, no worries," he says and leaves.

Mr. Kelp shuts the door behind him, and I can't help but wonder if he and Mr. Ward have something going on. I push the thought aside.

"How can I help you?" Mr. Kelp asks, his expression a mix of annoyance.

I take a deep breath, not sure how to start but knowing I have to get this off my chest.

"Okay," I blurt, "I was at the coffee shop last night." I pause, looking at him. "I know you know what I mean when I say that."

He looks stunned, his face paling slightly. So maybe... he didn't recognize me?

"Why are you saying this?" he demands.

I swallow hard, twisting my fingers in my hands. "I need to stay."

A bitter smile creeps across his face "You think you're so smart, but it's not up to me." He snaps leaning forward so that the space between us eerily.

I steady my trembling hands and force my gaze

upward. "You have power here, your wife's the chair. You can make a difference, your opinion matters." I say, my tone firm despite the pounding of my heart.

He steps closer to me, filling the small space between us. His eyes bore into mine as he tilts his head, and he challenges,

"And if not, what are you going to do?" His voice low and menacing, towering over me, looking down at me. I'm shaking, but I have to keep my composure.

"I'm sure you wouldn't want everyone to know you're blowing your business partner's son. That would embarrass your wife who just made chair, and make you look terrible; adultery and a closeted man? You'll maybe even look like a pedophile." I pause, my breath coming in ragged bursts, the accusation hanging heavy in the charges' silence. "Who knows how long you have been looking at your friend's son?"

He takes another brisk step forward, this time hitting the wall with the side of his fist. "Watch your fucking mouth!" he hisses at me.

I jump and see that he is away from the door. I hurry toward the door. "I don't want this, and I don't think that, I just need to stay, sorry I just— it's Brent he stole my idea right from under me. I swear I was prepared. He just completely threw me off. I just need to stay! That's all," I say my voice trembling in fear as I dart out, not looking back.

I go out the back of the building to the subway on the way out. I still see Brent's truck. In the same spot. Once I get on the subway. I catch my breath when it finally starts moving. Once I settle in, I let out a deep sigh, then a small chuckle. I can't believe I just did that. But I had to; there was no other way. They would have sent me home otherwise. I'm so glad I took the time to dig deeper into the coffee shop and prepare for my conversation with Mr. Kelp after my presentation. I had searched up Kauai Coffee, where I saw him the other night. It's a relatively new place, just two years old. The social media pages were full of pictures of their coffee and baked goods, but nothing too revealing.

Then, I found an article about the grand opening, with a picture of the owner, Bob Michael, and his son, Patrick, cutting the ribbon. Patrick looked to be in his early twenties. As I scroll further down, there was a picture of Mr. Kelp—he must be a partner or a good friend of the family.

I scroll back up to the picture of Patrick. Then it clicks: I recognize his legs from the coffee shop. He has a large scar running from his ankle to his knee. I later found his Instagram account. Turns out, the scar is from a surfing accident in Hawaii last year. He's a University of Hawaii Manoa alumni with a nice tan and frosted tips, his long wavy hair giving him a surfer vibe. He's cute.

I can still remember the look on his face when I screamed in the coffee shop. It looked like he saw a ghost. I wonder what Mr. Kelp might be telling him—maybe that he and Kathy are separated, or even getting a divorce? I'm dying to know how long this affair has been going on, and why the coffee shop of all places? Wouldn't he worry about being caught by someone? What if his father walked in?

Part of me wonders if I should say something to Patrick, but I'm still unsure. I go to my Instagram to make sure I'm logged into the right account, then send him a friend request, just in case.

The next few days go by smoothly. I haven't seen Mr. Kelp since our conversation. I don't know whether that's a good thing or a bad thing. Brent's been avoiding me, giving me strange looks every now and again. We're still working in the same digital marketing section, but now that the internship is full, they've assigned a site supervisor to each of us. Two interns left, and I couldn't help but notice how differently they reacted.

One was a tall girl named Jessica, and the other was a short, stocky guy named Oliver. Mr. Kelp made the announcement in front of everyone. When Oliver started packing up his stuff, I could see the sadness on his face. I'm sure he cried on the way home. Jessica, on the other hand, seemed unfazed. She looked rich—always in designer clothes, carrying expensive bags, and wearing Cartier rings. She'll be just fine. Now that there are an even number of interns and site supervisors we are all going to get paired.

My site supervisor's name is Ray. Ray looks like he's

twenty-five, with clear, smooth skin. I get nervous when Karen, the other manager, introduces us. He turns to me with a big smile, shakes my hand, and then I sit down beside him in his cubicle. With about 100 cubicles with huge monitors and keyboards. The monitor in the right corner of the room is to track what everyone is doing. Like when they're on calls and for how long. I look down at Ray's desk. He has funny bobbleheads and framed pictures of cats in ties. I now know we are going to get along beautifully. Maybe I will have a great time here.

Ray talks about the project he's working on that needs to be ready by next Monday. While he's talking, I'm just staring at him. He's beautiful in an unconventional way. He has big dark brown, almost black eyes, that kind of bug out of his head. A butt chin, with a defined jaw, full lips, and long eyelashes. A five o'clock shadow and a nose ring. I also see tattoos peeking out of his sleeves. He has dark skin, a slim athletic build, but is really tall, making him seem skinnier than he is. He's gorgeous. He has stopped talking, looking at me blankly. I think he has asked me a question. I haven't been listening.

"Sorry, um...what did you say I totally blanked, I haven't had my coffee yet this morning, sorry." I laugh as my face grows red. That is a lie. I have a coffee, and it's to the left of me. I hope he doesn't notice. He looks at the coffee. I look at it as well. Then we look at each other.

"I- I- haven't finished it."

He giggles. "It's fine," he says.

"But what I was saying is that I need you to do the

research like you did for the brand Sunday Best you
spoke about. I like how you related it to your life and
experiences. That's why I picked you. That's something
that is priceless: the ability to relate, the human experi-
ence of it all, speaks to everyone. I have a meeting with
the brand on Monday. I need a full report of their brand
for the past five to ten years. Could you do that for me? I
need you to include pictures, articles, etc."

Oh? Did he say he *picked* me!? I'm trying to hold my
composure. Once he establishes the business, he asks me
where I'm from and other things. I found out we were
both from Texas.

"Yeehaw," I say. He just smiles and shakes his head
at me. He asks how I'm liking New York and the
company. I tell him this has always been my dream.
Then I ask him how long he's been in New York City. He
tells me he has been in New York and with the company
for two years.

"Oh wow, okay, what are some of your favorite spots
to go to? We were planning to go out this weekend." I say.
Look at me flirting, I'm so smooth, with my soft
launch/potential invite. I'm sure we probably can't date
publicly, but we can easily sneak around. The thought of
that sends chills down my spine. I can't stop smiling.

"Um, let me think, oh me and my boyfriend love
going to Notorious Lounge, The Alibi for drinks, and
Krab King Korner if you like seafood," Ray says.

Boyfriend? Oh wow, of course, all the hot guys are
married, gay, or assholes. Maybe he's bisexual? I might

still have a chance! Oh, never mind he has a boyfriend, well at least he's not married. I just smile and nod.

"Thank you. I'm going to have to check those out!"

We continue working, making small talk here and there. I get kind of bored and start looking around to see where Athena is. I see her talking to Brent alone. What could they be talking about? I see her leaning forward, laughing, grabbing his arm. Brent is not funny like that. Is she flirting with him? That bitch, she knows I like him. Of course he prefers her, he's smiling too. They talk for about five more minutes. As she walks away, we make eye contact. I turn away, sighing. Today I'm confronting Brent. I can't wait to see what he's got to say for himself.

I tell Ray I have to go to the bathroom. He nods at me while still working on his computer. Knowing Athena planned to go out tonight, I went to freshen up. I check my makeup to see if it has stayed in tack.

I go for a simple look every day, using coral blush that compliments my brown skin, bronzer to accentuate my cheekbones, contour to make my round nose appear narrower, a touch of mascara, and a red-tinted lip gloss. I have my hair in a cute claw clip, with my curly strands of hair out to frame my face. I look good. I have really grown into my looks.

Even now I have a nice, slim, hourglass figure.

It only took twenty-two years but I'll take it. Not that everything is about my looks. I know I offer so many other important things to the world, like my intelligence, work ethic, compassion, etc. But when you're a woman, society acts as if you owe them beauty. If you're not beautiful, then you're nothing. I hate that my looks have dictated my life. It's something I learned early in life as a little girl. But now that it is apparent that I am attractive, I get treated somewhat differently.

Once I leave the bathroom, I see all the interns have been released. I checked my watch, and it is only two p.m. I guess we got let out early because it's Friday. Wow, one week down already, and I feel like I'm doing good. I grab my things, and Ray tells me to have a good night and reminds me we are supposed to be back for noon tomorrow since we have deadlines to work on. I then try to hurry to catch up to Athena to ask her about the weekend plans.

When I walk outside, I see Brent. He's digging into his backseat. Why does he always park in the back of the building that far? I always walk out the back because I enjoy walking this way to the subway. It is the long way but I do it because I want to feel like a local. I get to see all the little shops and all the New Yorkers rushing to get somewhere.

I head in his direction, mustering up the courage to confront him. Why would he do that? Was he trying to embarrass me? Or did he just use me as a leg-up? He jeopardized my place at the company, my future, fucking prick. I still can't believe that coward he can't even look me in the eye. Well, now, he's going to have to.

"Hey!" I blurt. "Do you want to tell me what the fuck your problem is?"

He jumps as he hears me yell at him. He then backs out and puts his elbow out to lean on his truck. As he does that, I get a whiff of his cologne or body wash. It smells good. The first three buttons of his shirt are unbuttoned revealing his muscled chest, and his sleeves are rolled up. It's getting warmer every day now. Thank God, I hate the cold. He's now looking at me smirking.

"You know what's funny? I was going to ask you the same thing."

I'm so upset. Why is he not taking me seriously? "What are you talking about?"

"You and Mr. Kelp, I heard you guys yelling at each other the other day. What's that all about?" I'm shocked at how he heard me whispering. I thought I ran out before anyone could hear.

"That's none of your business! Why did you steal my pitch?"

He's quiet now and I look in his trunk and back seat. There is a blanket and pillow and so many bags, trash bags and suitcases. *Is he living in his car?* He sees me looking and shuts his car door. He furrowed his eyebrows looking angry, or as if he's trying to cover his embarrassment.

"I didn't steal your pitch okay what you told me was nowhere near ground breaking. And more importantly what you're doing is illegal, you know, blackmail?" He scoffs.

"Yeah, when I went to grab my jacket. I overheard you and Mr. Kelp. Um, I'm kind of impressed. I didn't think you had it in you. Lil' Texan, but you know, what if everyone finds out that he's fucking little coffee shop boy, then your angle won't really work right? Or better yet, I'll get on his good side and say that I know you're a liar. You don't even have any proof, do you? What a rookie move."

I don't know what to say. I just move my head to look at the back of his truck.

"Are you homeless?" I say, narrowing my eyes at him.

"No.... I'm in between places right now, moving. I actually just found a new place to stay, thanks to you," he says, raising his eyebrows, as if he just thought of a brilliant idea.

"What—what are you talking about?" I contest shaking my head.

"I'll keep your secret; let you blackmail our boss. I might even help you, give you a few pointers. It is obvious you can use the help. What do you say?" He taps his finger on the hood of the car, a mischievous smirk on his lips.

I step back, crossing my arms defensively. "What? No." I retort, my tone edged with disbelief as I glance around.

Brent relaxes into a confident grin. "I'll say on the couch I work nights so you won't even know I'm there." He says.

My irritation flares as I snap, "What, you can't move in with me? Why didn't you tell them you had nowhere to stay? They paid for my room." I throw my hands up, my eyes flashing with incredulity.

Brent rolls his eyes and shrugs, leaning back on his truck with casual nonchalance. "That's because you're from Texas genius. I'm a local. I didn't even know they did that, and I used my old address on my paperwork. But that's neither here nor there. Do we have a deal or not?" His voice firm, and he leans forward, his gaze locked on mine.

My heart starts pounding as I stand rooted to the spot, my thoughts a jumble of worry and desire. I don't see a way out of this situation. I scan the parking lot, feeling suddenly exposed. Brent's proud self-assured smile sends a thrill through me—even as doubts churn in my stomach. He's so *sexy*. Oh, my goodness. I can't live with him. What if I snore? He's going to have to see me all ugly after I wake up, and share a bathroom? Oh, no. How did I get myself into this? This is so stupid. But I think I don't have a choice.

Finally, I muster a shaky smile and cross my arms tighter. "Um, okay, yes—only, only if you apologize.... yeah." My words come out rushed and unsure.

He immediately scoffs, his jaw clenching. "No." His tone is icy and for a moment the air between us seems to freeze.

I take a deep breath, stepping closer until we are nearly inches apart. "Well, okay, we can both get fired. I'll move back to Texas. No problem, I'll just work there. I don't care. And you can stay homeless. I'll expose you. I'll tell them that you lied on your paperwork, I'll suggest you have submitted fake documents. I'll make sure they investigate you. I'll call and email them every day." I say my voice low and concisely.

Brent's eyes widen, and he tightens his jaws and glances around. Surely, I've stumped him. Then, with a reluctant chuckle, he shakes his head.

"Okay." He murmurs his tone softening into a quiet, almost defeated, apology. "Sorry."

I'm winning. I get a sudden thrill. I tilt my head, my smile wry and challenging as I ask "Sorry for what, exactly?" My words are light but carry amusement.

He tilts his head back, locking his gaze with mine, as if to say, *really?* I can't help but laugh.

"All right, whatever. I'm tired of standing here arguing with your dumb-ass," I say as I open the door of his truck climbing into the passenger seat.

"Oh, really I'm the—" he says.

"No, I'm joking, but no really, why do you park where everyone can see you?" I shot him a look.

"No one saw me but you, I'm guessing you can recognize me from so far away, because you stare at me all the time." He says matter-of-factly.

I gasp. "No, I don't!" I'm mortified. I can't believe he just said that.

He thinks he's so funny.

"Oh, my God. No, I think it's just because your forehead is enormous. It's hard to miss. It reflects light and everything," I say waving my hands dramatically. He actually doesn't have a big forehead at all. He has a really cute perfect forehead.

"Ohhhh, okay, so that's it," he says as he looks at me, laughing even harder. I turn up the radio to drown out his laughter. Cheeks red. I laugh at myself.

"Take this right, then the next right at the light. First apartment on the left," I say.

"You can't walk in with me. People from the company live here. We're not supposed to have anyone staying with us, and Athena lives five doors down."

"Okay.... so how am I getting up?" he says. I pointed at the fire escape. "Oh, wow, what about my bags?"

"You'll figure it out, big boy, apartment 1021," I say as I hop out of the truck.

Once I walk into the lobby of our apartments, I see Athena talking to some older man. He looks about forty-five, he's short with gelled back hair. He looks like he's a Wall Street guy. I walk toward the elevator.

Athena sees me and says, "Oh hey, Karma, I've been looking for you!" She runs up to me, leaving the man she was speaking with like we're best friends. She grabs my arms. "Oh, thank you just in time. That man would not leave me alone." She rolls her eyes, looking exhausted.

"Oh really? Y'all seem like you are getting along," I say.

"Yeah? Good. I have to keep making it seem like that or he'll stop sending me money." She laughs, shaking her head.

"Girl, it's a full-time job. Men love to act like little babies that you have to cradle."

Is she a sugar baby or a prostitute? I guess that's how

she gets all these cute expensive clothes, jewelry, her hair and nails done.

"I'm no sugar baby, though, if that's what you're thinking. I mean, I'm not giving up any sugar. He just likes to talk, you know? Poor bastard," she says as she applies more lip gloss to her already glossy lips. She's so pretty.

"Okay, soooo!" she says in an excited tone. "What are we doing tonight?"

"I'm not sure, I don't really have any good clubbing clothes to wear and I have to do all this research for Ray," I say.

"Uhhhhh, Karma, come on you have so much time to do that. Right now, we need to find where all the rich, hot guys go to party, I heard the Knicks are playing a home game tonight. I bet they're going out after," she says as she looks at her phone.

"Oh yay! My friend just texted me saying everyone's going to Hypnotic tonight! We have to go! We have to find you something to wear." She's looking me up and down.

"I think we're the same size. We will find you something! I'll meet you in your room around seven, okay?"

Nodding, I remember Brent. I almost forgot about him.

"Um, no, I'll meet you at yours so you don't have to drag all your stuff over, you know?" I say nervously.

"Okay, yeah," she says as the elevator lands on our floor. "See you in a little." She walks into her apartment; she smiles at me as she closes the door.

I smile back and once I get in my apartment, I see

Brent, he's inside already sitting on the couch. I jumped; he scared me.

"How did you get in already? God, you almost gave me a heart attack!"

"Eh," he says as he shrugs, "I just wiggled the window around a little. I was tired of waiting," says Brent.

I just stare at him, kind of turned on, kind of taken aback. He sits slouched on the couch, running his fingers through his dark curly hair, looking up at me.

"I have to do some research for a bit, then I'm going out. So don't bother me. There is an extra comforter and pillow in the closet," I spit.

"I'm about to leave for work. In a little, I'll be back in a few hours. Can you leave the fire escape open?" he says.

"Yes, well, does it even matter, you'd just break in anyway?"

"You're right, but please just save me the hassle. I'm going to be exhausted," he says, smiling at me with his pretty pink lips.

"Sure, what do you even do?" I ask.

He put his head on his hand. "I'm a—uh, stripper. You know, um, like magic mike." He points at himself. "I'm Mike. With magic." He sings, 'I got the magic stick, mhmhmh,' in a sing-song voice. We just look at each other. I can't help but giggle. What a dork.

"You don't believe me?" He pulls out his yellow hard hat helmet. "Why else would I have one of these?" he says as he puts it on his head.

"Construction?" I suggest.

"No, of course not," he says as we chuckle. He has such a beautiful smile, when he laughs you can see his bottom teeth that are slightly crooked, so adorable. Wow, I could just rip his clothes off right now. No, he's already shown me twice. I can't trust him. My smile drops.

"Kidding. I am in construction. Anyway, I'm going to do my work. See you later". His smile fades as well. I think he can feel how my mood just changed.

"All right, no problem. I'll be gone in a minute. Just have to change," he says. I point to let him know where the bathroom is. I close my bedroom door behind me, plop belly-first on my bed and scream into my pillow. What the fuck am I doing? My phone dings again. It's him, Lucas. I can't talk to him right now. I don't even know how to.

Maybe I just have to delete my social media accounts and block his number. Be done with it all. "FUCK!" I scream again in my pillow. Unable to focus right now to do my work, so much is going on. I hear a knock at the door. Maybe it's Athena. My eyes widened. Oh, she can't be here, she'll see Brent.

Per Mr. Kelp, the Intern Program Manager, we are not allowed to fraternize with members employed here. I can't tell her. That would just make everything worse, and I don't trust her. I jump out of bed, open my door, and look back and forth for Brent. I think he left already.

Okay, now I can breathe. I go to open the door. It's Athena.

She smiles at me and says, "Come on girl we ain't got all day."

I look at my watch. "It's only six o'clock."

"Yeah, but I'm hungry and I have to do my makeup and find you an outfit. We got a lot of shit to do, girl."

I laugh, grab my purse, and go to her room. I love the decorations in the hallways with the burgundy printed carpets, and the expensive textured cream and white wallpaper.

Once I walk into Athena's place, I'm surprised about how big it is. It is twice the size of mine. It looks like a presidential suite. She has a huge living room and kitchen that looks so modern with marble countertops and white leather furniture and a flat-screen TV. Her view is even better than mine. How come she got this room?

"Wow, your place is sooo much better than mine!"

Athena looks at me, shocked. "Really? I wonder why?" I just look around her apartment in awe. Why does she have everything I want? Well, at least she's willing to share. I look around her room. She has a walk-in closet with over twenty designer bags on the shelves and so many outfits with the tags still on, Louis Vuitton, Versace, and Chanel shoes and perfumes. How rich is she? Then I see a check book open in her closet.

"You have a checkbook? What are you, sixty?" I laugh,

skimming through it. Seeing a woman's name Shirley Tipton on the checkbooks.

Athena speed walks toward me snatching it away from me and says, "It's my grandpa's, he has dementia. So, I'm in charge of his finances, you know, to pay the mortgage and stuff."

Shirley? That's not a man's name. Is it? She quickly changes the subject.

"You know something I realized earlier. I was just going to call you, but I don't have your number. Let me see your phone." I hand her my phone.

"What's your passcode?" she asks.

I hesitate. "Um, my birthday is 0707," I say.

She gasps. "Ohhh you're a Cancer, huh? That makes so much sense,"

I chuckle. "Why do you say that? What's your sign?"

"Sagittarius."

"I don't know. That's just your vibe. You seem shy and innocent," she says, narrowing her eyes at me with a goofy, slight smile, "But I can tell you've got some tricks up your sleeve."

"Oh, you have no fucking clue," I say in an enigmatic tone.

She giggles. "Karma, you're a fucking hoot," and goes to walk-in closet and says, "this is what I was thinking for you." She holds up the set with a black halter that's cropped and open in the middle and a black matching mini skirt.

"Hot, right? I felt like you're more modest. Daddy wouldn't like that type," she says with a dramatic southern accent. "But we aren't buying drinks tonight and I'm planning on not remembering anything in the morning, you know? So, we have to dress the part!" I'm excited. I need a fun night out.

"Okay yea, that's cute. Have you ever worn it?" I see the tags are still on.

"No, I got it like two days ago. I was gonna wear it, but I think it'll look better on you. You'll be able to fill it out more," she says as she moves her shoulders back and forth while she pokes her lips out like a duck. She's so animated. Our bodies are kind of similar. She's thinner and taller. She's like 5 '9" and has a body like a swimsuit model, long legs, curvy torso, and an A cup chest. I'm 5 '7" with a slim hourglass figure and a B cup chest.

After I get changed, she puts on this corset top that makes her chest pop and low-rise jeans with a star sewn in the backs. She looks so cool. I'm worried the burrito I had for lunch was going to pop out my top.

We do our makeup and chit-chat and get to know each other. She's actually really funny and easy to be around. We tell each other funny stories about our childhood, how we both grew up as only an only child. And how obsessed we were with boy bands and gossip magazines as a kid. We talked about our favorite shows and songs. We actually have so much in common. I'm having a lot of fun. This is what I wanted. I'm happy. She calls the car as we get in the elevator. She tells me she has this friend she met yesterday that she invited to come with.

"Forgot to tell you her name, Kendall. She's an intern too. We sit beside each other. Her supervisor is such a dick; he's kind of cute though. She's going to meet us downstairs."

"Oh, cool," I say. I see Kendall walking toward us. She's petite, five nothing, with warm brown skin and honey-blonde dreads that cascade down her back. As she gets closer, her striking features become more apparent, she's so pretty. With her nose and eyebrow piercing, and one of the biggest, widest smiles I have ever seen. Her outfit, a tube top and baggy paint-distorted pants make her look like a Pinterest photo. She exudes a cool, effortlessly stylish New York vibe.

She walks up smiling big, saying hi, and opening her arms to hug. I can tell we're going to get along already. The car pulls up. We all get in, Athena's catching Kendall up telling her where we're going, and that she invited the boys, which she didn't even tell me.

Then one of the old boy band songs from ages ago, that me and Athena talked about plays on the radio. When I hear it, I exclaim, "Ohhhh, I love this song!" I smile and look over to them.

Kendall says, "I never really got into boy bands as a kid, never really liked him."

I gasp dramatically and look at Athena to back me up, Athena says, "Me neither."

I look at her confused. "What didn't you just—" *We just talked about being obsessed with them in her room.*

She ignores me, shrieks at her phone and says, "My friend just got us in VIP! I hear a lot of pro athletes show up there. This is gonna be so fun!"

When we got to the club, Athena runs up to the front of the line, which had to be about a hundred people long. We run after her. By the time we get there, the bouncers open the rope for her so we could all go through.

As we walked into the club, the music is pounding. Throngs of people are dancing, laughing, and drinking. Athena takes my hand and leads me up to the second floor, where the music is a little different, a little softer with more rap. I noticed a few of the guys wear big watches, have chains around their necks, or are wearing suits. There were also twice as many women as men.

Athena goes up and hugs one of the men in a suit. He is young and wealthy-looking. I wonder how they know each other, probably how she knows all those other men. Does she do sex work, or is she famous online, or maybe it's old money? Her dad might be rich and have a lot of business friends. I'll find out, eventually.

Athena introduces us and he buys us a bottle. We all take shots and then Athena takes the bottle and tells us to follow her when the man turns his head. We rushed down the stairs and when we get down them, I asked her, "What was that about?"

"He was getting on my nerves. He wouldn't leave me

alone. You see him? Huh? He kept touching me. Such a weirdo!"

Her reaction surprised me because I thought she seemed to like him. They hugged and kissed a few times. I turn to Kendall. She just shrugs. Athena gets more shot glasses from the bar and hands them to us. I don't really drink unless it's socially. I hate the taste of alcohol, but being tipsy is fun. It helps me not be shy. We jump around and dance.

They are playing old pop hits that all three of us know the words to. With the number of shots I took, I'm really starting to feel it. A little too much now. I mean, I know I'm a lightweight, but I'm more than drunk. My head is spinning.

To avoid focusing on that, I just keep dancing. God, I'm so out of it. Everything's so blurry I'm dizzy, but I feel kind of good. I laugh, and so does Kendall. We keep dancing together, then I look around and see that Athena is not by us anymore. Then I spot her up at the bar, staring at us, motionless.

Then I see the boys from Introspection, Brent and Ryan. They walk up to Athena and the look on her face immediately changes. She smiles and hugs Brent, which sends a pang of jealousy through me. I grab Kendall and head over there to talk to them. I see that guy that Athena was talking to upstairs, comes down from the second floor. "Oh, look there's your boyfriend," I say half-jokingly.

Athena shoots me a daggered look furrowing her eyebrows. "What are you talking about?"

"The guy from the second floor that you were hanging out with. The one that gave us the bottle," I say sheepishly. I don't know what I have said wrong. She keeps looking at me like she's furious.

"I don't have a boyfriend, you fucking weirdo. Why are you saying this, because they are here?" She points toward the boys.

"Karma, you're such an attention whore and it's insufferable. If you want to fuck them so bad no one's standing in your way," she says as she steps back dramatically. Hands in the air.

"I didn't..." I begin.

"You didn't what? Oh my gosh, you're slurring your words already. You really need to learn how to handle your liquor. You're being sloppy."

I just looked at her shocked. The boys' eyes widen with their mouths opened, taken aback. I feel my cheeks grow red. I want to apologize. I was just kidding, but she looks really mad at me now. Feeling like I'm going to throw up, I turn away and run to the bathroom. Everything spins. *I'm just drunk. I need to calm down*, I tell myself. But what was that about? Why did she say that? I feel like I can't even go home right now. I can't even face Brent. Wow, he probably thinks I'm obsessed with him.

I'm losing my balance and I cry so hard I throw up. *What is wrong with me? I don't know why I'm so out of it. I gasp. What if that man spiked the bottle? Oh, no way. What if this feeling doesn't stop?* There is no way I could have been roofied. Athena gave me these drinks, but she also got it from that man. What if he had roofied the bottle? Then I hear someone banging on the door saying my name, while I'm lying on the floor by the toilet panicking. Then everything goes dark.

9

Diary entry- 5 years ago

WE DON'T TALK about what happened last night. In the morning my dad just brings an enormous duffel bag of money that he stole from them I'm guessing. Then grabs an empty duffel bag and puts half of the money in bundles, of what I'm guessing is about a quarter million dollars in each. He zips it up and puts it on the hotel bed.

"This is yours. Okay, you're going to take this and go to college. Okay? This should be enough for your tuition, food, your room and board. Yeah, it's all here," he says.

"I want to stay with you, Dad. I don't want to go to college." It would be nice to have someone around, especially since everyone else in our family has left or doesn't want to be with me.

"I'll always be checking in on you, you can always count on me. I'm so sorry for what I put you through. I hate what happened. I was too careless, you deserve better, and to have an actual future. We have to go now because I have to get rid of the car."

"I haven't even applied."

He says that he already did months ago on my behalf. "You got accepted in so many schools, but I knew NYU would be your favorite." And he was right. I talked about how beautiful New York is, and how much I wanted to go.

Tears stream down my face as he gently pats my back and tells me we have to leave now, to make the train to the airport before it's too late.

We get in the car, and he talks about how he's so proud of me and how excited he is for this new chapter in my life. I feel a mix of emotions—excitement, sadness, fear, but deep down, I know this is what's best. I still don't know why my dad owed that man money. I don't want to ask, in fear it would ruin the mood.

Before we part ways, he gives me my ID that he has kept in his wallet since I started working with him. And the bag of money, which is heavier than I thought. Then he gives me an envelope. I attempt to open it and he stops me and tells me to read it on the train. I say okay, we hug, and he tells me he loves me. He tears up and apologizes again. I tell him it's okay then he kisses me on my forehead and says goodbye. I get on the train. Once I take a seat, I can still see him as I look out the window. He's waiting for us to leave, I open the letter, it reads:

I'm proud of you and will love you forever. You

are my strong and beautiful daughter. Make the
best of what you have won.
   Bye Bunny,
   Love Dad.

My heart sinks, and I look back. He's still there, smiling and waving.

He knows.

10

Karma

I WAKE up in my bed with my clothes still on and a throbbing headache. I look around my room trying to puzzle together what happened last night. Then everything comes together. I remember my fight with Athena. What was that about? I sob. Then I realized I don't remember how I got home and I don't know if Brent's here or not.

So, I cry quietly and then my stomach turns again and my mouth gets watery. *Oh no*, I run to the bathroom and throw up. Then I feel a little better, well, my stomach at least. I'm feeling nervous about how everything will play out today. As I get from the bathroom and look at my phone and see if anyone has texted me and then I check the time it's 9 a.m.

I hear Brent walk in through the front door. I close my bedroom door behind me. I feel my eyes fill up with water. I can't believe what Athena said last night.

Now Brent is going to be acting weird toward me. I get under the covers and put my face into the pillow. There is no way I can go to work today. I hear Brent's footsteps grow closer to the door. He knocks. My heart drops.

"Hey, Karma, I got some breakfast, coffee and some headache medicine. I don't know if you're awake or not, but I'll just leave it by the door," I hear him say as he drops the bags at the door.

Well, at least he's handling this well. I thought he was going to be awkward. Maybe he just feels bad for me. Wow. But that's really sweet of him. I wonder what Kendall thinks? Just when I thought everything was going well. I hear Brent leave, probably to go back to Introspection. It's a bit early though to leave, they told us we don't need to be in until noon, but maybe he wants to give me some space.

I get dressed. Now that I think about it, I don't even see Athena for most of the day anymore. Since we're in different sections, I can make new friends. I'll be fine. I grab the breakfast from in front of my door and I open it, its grilled cheese and a piece of avocado toast with sun-dried tomatoes and bacon. With coffee and some orange juice. My heart gushes. Wow, that was so nice of him. Does he like me or just pity me? I'm fine with either at the moment. I eat, get dressed, and then do some quick makeup.

Although I rush, I actually arrive early. It's Saturday so we got to come in late. A lucky mistake, I guess. We are having to work this weekend because of the urgent deadline. I immediately went in looking for Ray. Hopefully, he's here early as well. I need to see a familiar face that wasn't there to witness me last night. I find Ray in the break room. Thank God.

"Hi, Ray, how are you?"

Ray looks back at me blankly. He takes a second to recognize me. His expression lightens, and he smiles with two sugar packets in his hand as he's in the middle of making his morning coffee.

"Good morning, I'm good, what about you?" he asks.

He looks good today. He's wearing off-white slacks, a white linen button-down with the top two buttons unbuttoned, small gold hoop earrings. With a gold chain and a few gold bracelets and some brown loafers. He's so handsome and well-dressed. His boyfriend is so lucky, I wonder what he looks like. Ray is looking at me as if he's waiting for me to respond. I think I zoned out while I was checking him out.

"Sorry, what was that? I didn't sleep well last night." I chuckle.

He giggles just to be polite. "I said Mr. Kelp is here today. He's been asking for you."

My face immediately drops. My heart races. "What, um, about what?" I say, trying to sound calm.

"I'm not sure, he found out you'll be working under me, and he said he needed to speak with you. Maybe it's about him liking your pitch." he slaps my shoulder playfully. "Don't be nervous, he looks all big and bad but he's a decent guy."

I might throw up again. What would he need to talk to me about?

"Are you okay? You are looking gray in the face?" Ray says with a concerned look on his face.

"Yeah, sorry, I just didn't sleep well last night ha-ha —" I tried to laugh it off. "I'll see you over there. I'm going to see what he wants."

I run to the restroom. I open the stall and hide by sitting on the toilet with my legs up. How long can I stay here till Mr. Kelp forgets about me? What could he possibly have to say to me? Is he going to fire me? I will let his wife know what he does if he tries to do that, but then I'd just have to go back home. What good would that do me? I can't hide in this bathroom all day. Maybe just a few more minutes.

After about twenty minutes, I get up. I have a plan. Once I do, I hear two people come into the bathroom. I sit back down quietly and pick my feet up. Recognizing their voices, I can't face them right now. It's Athena and someone else, I can tell it's her by her laugh. It's very high-pitched and carries.

"Can you believe he found her in the bathroom passed out last night?" Athena says.

"Who found her? I barely remember anything from last night," the other girl says, sounds *like Kendall*.

"Brent! He literally picked her up from the bathroom like a white knight." She laughs. "So embarrassing. Do you think she is going to show up today? I know I wouldn't," says Athena.

What a bitch. While I'm in the fetal position on the toilet, I feel my eyes fill up with water. I thought I was making friends, but they're just making fun of me. I didn't even drink a lot. I sink into myself. Then I hear her heels come toward my stall. She knocks on the door and asks who's in there? I pop up and open the door. Scaring her.

She gasps really loudly and puts a hand on her chest and steps back.

"Karma, what the fuck are you doing in here, goofy? I'm glad you showed up. I know you had a rough night last night, are you okay?" she says in a giggle, like I didn't just hear her talking shit about me.

"Don't tell me you were throwing up again? See, I gave you a little bar to help you loosen up. I didn't think it'd make you go all crazy." She moves her hands all dramatically.

Did she say a bar like Xanax? She drugged me? Why is she acting like this is normal? She's the reason I got so sick.

"What?" I say.

"What?" she mimics me. "Come on I was doing you a favor girl, I single-handedly got Brent to take you home, you're welcome... it's not even a big deal! See, you cleaned up nice, you look hot even after all that. I knew you had it in you babe!" She turns around to reapply her cherry red lip gloss.

"I'll see you later," Athena says as she walks out flippantly. Like she didn't just confess that she drugged me and I didn't just witness her talking shit about me.

Kendall looks at me confused.

"You didn't know about the bars? She told me you kept asking for one and you just overdid it."

"No! I've never even taken a bar. I barely even know what that is," I say.

She looks at me like she is not sure if she believes me. Has Athena told more lies about me? I huff at her and shake my head.

"It's okay, you look good. That's all that matters. Just chill out. Also, Mr. Kelp is looking for you. I'll see you later, all right?"

"Okay, yeah, I know," I say, burying my face in my hands. I try to fix myself up and give myself a pep talk in the mirror. If he wants to fire me, I won't have anything else better to do than make his life a living hell. I have my career at stake, but he has his life at stake. My odds are better than his. When I get to his office, the door is open. I walk in. Mr. Kelp is talking on the phone. He looks up at me and says,

"Okay, yeah, I'm going to have to call you back later. Yeah, bye." He hangs up the phone just looking at me, staring at me, not breaking eye contact.

I don't falter in my eye contact. As it seems, he expects me to.

"Sit down," he says, gesturing his eye to the chair in front of his desk. I sit down, still keeping my bearing. "Take that smug look off your face. You know nothing."

"I—"

"No," he cuts me off. "What you need to do is stay out

of my fucking way and do your job. You don't have the upper hand here, you understand? You have no clue what you're talking about and no evidence, and just so you know, I don't pick who's going to stay. My wife does whatever the fuck she wants and if you try anything, I swear that would be the last thing you do."

Now I'm scared. He's so angry and did he just threaten to kill me? He did. He wouldn't. There are too many people to witness. He's making an empty threat. He committed adultery, not a crime. That makes him a cowardly pompous man. And Brent knows about this, I'll be fine. I sit up higher in my chair.

"Well, hopefully it won't have to come to that, sir. Have a good day," I say as I get up from my chair and walk out.

My hands are shaking and my heart rate is going fast. I did it. Everything's going to be fine. I giggle inside. I was worried about nothing. Athena doesn't hate me, but she is kind of crazy. Brent was sweet enough to take care of me. Was it out of pity or because he cares about me?

Ugh, the things I would do to him: sexy, caring and sweet. He's kind of a con artist though, a blackmailer and now I am too. I wonder what else he is capable of. He's also homeless. I wonder how that came to be. I realize I know little to nothing about this strange man that lives in my place. Later, I'll need to look him up. Now I'm back at Ray's desk. I have a chipper smile on my face as I say

"Hey, what's on the agenda for today?"

"You look like you're in a better mood. See, it wasn't all that bad, was it?"

"No, it went perfectly." I look at Ray. I'm curious if he's also Mr. Kelps type. I know he likes them young.

11

Diary entry 8 years ago

I REALIZED I'm different from people my age. For one thing, I'm sad all the time. I have been sad for a long while. Recently I've been searching online for what to do about it. One article suggested going to therapy or starting a journal if you're depressed. I can't do therapy. So now I'm writing. They said it's best to use a journal for all your burning thoughts and feelings.

So yeah, something that's really bugging me is that when me and my sister were younger, we looked like twins, although we're a year apart. (well, ten months to be exact). Now that we're in middle school, we look different. People call her the "pretty one" and I'm the "bigger one." I'm not even chubby, I just look chubby next to her. I hate being around her now.

At school, people always have to point it out and we don't even look that much alike. One person who doesn't do that is Kyle. He's in my math class and we sit by each other. It's only because of the seating chart. He's really cute and nice. He plays football, and he has a really cute smile. Yesterday we had to work together in groups and put our desks together. So, I sat right next to him! And our knees touched! He didn't move them either! He even smiled at me when he felt our knees touch.

He's so funny too! He was telling me stories about his friends falling at football practice

After class he walked me to my locker. Well, my locker is right next to the class. But still. He was walking with me until I got to my locker then he said he will see me later. Smiling and waving. I think he likes me!!!!!

12
Karma

A COUPLE of days have passed and everything has run pretty smoothly. Athena acts like nothing has happened, and so do the boys. I follow suit, I don't want to rehash everything, because I'm embarrassed and maybe she was just trying to help me have more fun and let loose. She knew I was kind of nervous. How is she sure I have a crush on Brent? Do I make it that obvious?

I don't have a crush, per se. I think he is hot. That's why I have also been trying my best to avoid him or make eye contact. Has Athena said something to him? But there's something off about him I can't figure out. I even tried looking him up everywhere first and last name on all social media platforms and nothing came up. I even googled him.

Then I believed maybe I wasn't spelling his name right, so I went through his bag while he was showering. I found his wallet, and I was spelling his last name wrong. I got a slight thrill looking through his bag, grabbed his ID, jumped in bed then got on my laptop, typed his name in correctly this time, Brent Ignacio, again I found nothing on social media. A few people with his name that definitely weren't him.

I then googled his name and a few things popped up, like his stats from football and basketball from high school. Nothing from college or anything. I go to the website with his stats. A picture of him pops up from his senior year. He looks so cute with his short haircut and no facial hair. Why can't I find anything? I need to find out his mother's name, brother, best friend, or something to fill in the blanks. Oh, Ryan! What's his last name... I remember it being a super generic last name: Smith, Johns, Anderson, yes Anderson! Yes, I type in Ryan Anderson into Facebook and a million people pop up.

Okay, I need to narrow this down by putting where he's from. Um, I forgot I know he's from the UK, but I'm not sure which country or town um. Whatever I type in the UK beside his name. Tens of thousands of people show up and none are remotely close to him. Ugh, this is going to be a lot harder than I thought. Oh! I know I'll just go back to Brent's varsity high school highlight's website and see what high school they went to.

Okay, yes, I found Lumber City High. I typed that in by Ryan's name. I found him! But to my disappointment, his profile is as generic as his last name. I double-check in on the right account and I friend him. I will find more information if we are friends. Although it looks like he hasn't been active in years, it is better than nothing. At least then I'd be able to see his friends that would inevitably be Brent's friends, girlfriends, ex-girlfriends, etc.

I do the same on Instagram and Twitter. Although I found Brent on Twitter, the last time he was active was about ten years ago and he has two posts. Who doesn't post on social media? This makes everything more difficult for me. I need to know more. I hear the shower stop and I rush back to the living room to put his ID back into his wallet.

When I get back to my room, I get a notification from Lucas and it says,

> I see you're online. Why won't you text me back? What's going on?!

My heart sinks. I'm so over this. I have better things now. That's something I don't want to do anymore. Right before I close my laptop, I see another notification

'*Kathy Kelp has accepted your friend request!*' I gasp. Yes, finally!

13

Diary entry- 8 years ago

DANI'S MOM is really sick. So, Dani comes over a lot now. She and my sister go out a lot. Dani is popular, and my sister wants to be popular. That's the only reason they hang out, and why she doesn't hang out with me anymore. Dani's boyfriend is a senior in high school so he drives them everywhere, to high school parties and stuff. They are in the ninth grade. I'm in eighth grade. But that's all they talk about now, boys and parties. They are so annoying.

My mom hurt herself a few days ago when she fell down the stairs or something when she was off with her boyfriend. Now she hasn't left her room in days. She just yells out to me to bring her food or wine. The school year is almost over. I can't wait for summer. My dad said he might pick us up to spend it with him! Yay!

14

Karma

THE NEXT DAY AFTER WORK, we have an office party with all the departments there at Introspection in the auditorium. It looks different. They put white cloth tables and chairs everywhere. Waiters walk around in all black. They got catering from this new Japanese restaurant, with sushi and drinks flying everywhere. We all go together with Athena, Kendall, and me.

Mr. Kelp greets us with a big smile on his animated face, as he throws his hands in the air.

"Hey, girl, welcome to the party! Best one of the year," he says slurring his speech, eyes wide. His wife is three feet away with a drink in her hand. She is talking to a few other wives; they all look like their old friends catching up. Kathy side-eyes him. She doesn't seem amused. We grab some champagne glasses and Kendall brings up how odd Mr. Kelp is acting. I don't enjoy talking about him.

"How many shots do you think Kelp has had?" Kendall says.

Athena raises her eyebrows. "More like how many lines? Man's got to be on something."

We giggle and meet a few of our colleagues' significant others and then I feel a tap on my shoulder, afraid it's Mr. Kelp, my shoulders tense up. I slowly turn around and it's Ray.

"Hey!" I say, relieved.

"Hey, this is Marcus, my boyfriend I was telling you about", says Ray. Marcus is a short man with pale skin, dirty blonde short hair, and round red cheeks. He looks so pleased to be here. I love him already.

"Hi! I'm Karma, nice to meet you, y'all make a lovely couple!"

Marcus blushes even more, which I didn't think was possible. He covers his mouth and says, "Oh wow, thank you! You look gorgeous. I love that outfit!" Marcus swings his hands around flamboyantly. He's adorable.

"Thank you! Y'all look amazing as well! I love y'all's coordinating outfits! So cute!" I say.

"He always asks what I'm wearing before we meet up to go to an event and I tell him. No, we are not matching today and he says I'm not trying to. I just want to see the vibe. So, I show him and then he ends up in an outfit almost identical or the same colors!" Ray says, rolling his eyes.

Even though he said he hates it, I know he's amused. Marcus shrieked with laughter and hits Ray's shoulder playfully covering his mouth while shaking his head, like a guilty toddler that thinks he's so clever.

"I don't do that, oh my goodness," Marcus says. We're all giggling.

"What are you drinking? I'm going to need like five of those." Ray says as he glances around eagerly.

I point over to the little bar area.

They head over there. Marcus says it's nice to meet me and I say the same. I look over my shoulder and Kendall and Athena aren't in eyesight, so I try to look around discreetly to not look like an absolute loser with no social skills and/or friends. I hate losing my friends at a party.

When in doubt I just run to the bathroom, I see the bathroom sign a few feet away and dart there. As I'm on my way, I see Kendall, thank God. "Hey! I was worried I'd lost you guys!" I say as I take a sip of my drink. Athena's on the right side of Kendall talking to a guy and a girl, both of which I don't recognize. Athena's glare at the girl makes me feel the tension. I wonder what's going on. What did I miss? I mean, I'm not surprised. Drama follows Athena wherever she goes.

A few days ago, she told me one of the older managers keeps touching her and making weird passes at her. I told her she needs to report to him, but she dismisses me when I say that. But she feels the need to let me know about it every other day. I don't understand her. The girl catches me staring at her.

She smiles and puts out her hand and says "Hi, I'm Dani, how are you?"

"Oh, hi. I'm Karma. I'm good. How are you?" I say as I shake her hand.

She's pretty, like a barbie with her shiny long blonde hair, big hazel eyes, wearing a light blue tube top, and floor length white flowy skirt.

"I grew up with Athena and her sister, Serena, in Jersey. We go way back. I was so shocked to see her here I almost didn't believe it!" She shoots a look at Athena.

"This is my boyfriend, Josh. He and Athena work right beside each other, apparently. Small world, huh?" She pans to Athena. "You know you look almost exactly the same from the last time I saw you, what you were only like fifteen/sixteen at the time?" she says, gleefully. "Guys, you want to know something crazy about her? She and her sister used to look almost identical! You could barely tell them apart once they hit high school!"

"What do you mean? You have a twin?" I say excitedly.

"No! Ha-ha, they are exactly like what? Ten months and a week apart. But before you could tell, because, no offense Serena was a late bloomer. She was chubby and didn't get boobs till like Sophomore year, after that everyone thought they were twins! Teachers, Athena's boyfriend, and their mother would get them confused. They almost fooled me too, sometimes. But it's nice to see that you're still so pigeon-toed! You can't even hide it in those heels!" She laughs.

"Dani," Josh says under his breath.

"What? No, it's endearing. We have an inside joke from when we were kids. It's funny, because no, they looked almost exactly the same and they dressed alike. It got kind of creepy."

I look toward Athena. She's not laughing. She's now glaring at Dani. I wonder what's going on.

Athena pulls her face into a fake smile and says, "Yeah, it was really nice seeing you. But um sorry I really have to pee; I'll catch up with you guys later!"

I follow her as I say. "Me too! Nice to meet you!" over my shoulder.

Once I get into the bathroom, I see Athena pacing back and forth, whispering to herself. I just stand there and once we make eye contact, she looks at me all wide-eyed and deranged. She darts toward me. Now we're only a few inches apart. I step back. She's scaring me.

"You think I can fuck her boyfriend?"

I'm startled "Um I—" she cuts me off.

"It's the way he looks at me. I know I can," she says as she nods, crossing her arms with wide-eyed pupils dilated.

"That fucking bitch I hate her!" she screams.

"What happened? Who is that?" I ask.

"It's just some fucking bitch that lived across the street of the house I grew up in. She was never even my friend. She was my sister's friend! How fucking dare she talk about my sister after what happened to her! What a sick bitch. She's so lucky I didn't punch her in the face UGH. I can't believe this. Can you?" she huffs at me.

"No oh my—what happened to your sister?" I ask. Athena turns to me now with a sorrowful look on her face, which is almost unrecognizable from her face of rage earlier.

"She died."

Athena puts her head in her hands and starts hysterically crying and I pat her on the back. She looks up at me and pats her face under her eyes, but I'm not sure any tears are coming out. She tells me she's still mourning her sister, and that Dani knows that.

"I can't be here. This is too much," she says. I watch her rush out as we leave the bathroom. Everyone sees her rush out as well. I go back to the group and tell them Athena got really upset about her sister and had to leave.

"What happened to her sister?" asks Kendall.

"She passed," I say.

Dani whips her head toward me and says. "No, Serena went missing. No one said she died. It has just been like over five years, so they gave up and she was *presumed dead*, which is not the same thing at all. And if you ask her mom—never mind." She shakes her head. "I don't know what happened, but it's really strange that's all. There is something wrong with that family and many people feel the same."

15

Diary entry- 8 years ago

MY DAD SAID he can't make it this summer just like last summer and the one before. I hate that I have to be stuck here, there is nothing to do in this town, and mom doesn't take us anywhere. My sister is going out with Dani more and more. I think they're best friends now.

My mom keeps yelling at my sister to take me with her. I tell her I don't want to hang out with them. Mom doesn't listen to me; she says that I need to get out of the house.

At first, my sister and I got annoyed, but it felt like old times, like when we were best friends. Now I figured out what they do all the time. They are at Dani's house, or at the park with boys smoking weed and drinking. I tried weed for the first time in an alley. I liked it; it made me feel less nervous. We did that and got a ride back home with Dani's boyfriend. His name is Michael, he has a pubey-like mustache, and drives a beat-up Ford truck that smells like cigarettes. Dani and my sister smoke those too. Each day, they'd threaten to kill me if I told our moms.

I'd say, "Why do you think I would do that? I'm doing the same thing?"

Then they would say I'm right and laugh.

Most days we get high or drunk, and go back to Dani's house and chill, watch reality TV or go on online chat rooms. We do it at Dani's because her mom is sick and always sleeps in her room. Dani has grown on me. She's pretty laid-back and cool. She says whatever's on her mind and she's pretty, witty, and funny. I see why she's popular. I also feel kind of bad for her.

She was telling us last weekend that they are running out of money. I asked her how she knew and she told me about all the letters in the mail. All the medical bills, expenses, and how there is a late rent past due. So, she doesn't know what's going to happen. My sister said she could move in with us. My mom wouldn't like that and where would she sleep? I want to help. I'm going to do some research tonight! I'll come up with a plan fast! I have to figure something out!

16

Karma

I DON'T KNOW what to think about Athena. All this is super weird. I want to ask her more about it, but I don't want to pry. What if she just lies to me? She's done it before many times. I recall asking her if she had any siblings and her saying no. I even told her how weird it is growing up with no siblings, and she agreed. Well, now, I guess that would make her an only child. *Why is she saying her sister is dead and not missing? Does she know something the cops don't?* I text her to ask her if she's okay and if she wants to talk about it. I don't get a response.

When I get to my apartment complex, I put my ear to Athena's door, to try and see if she's home. I hear nothing, not even the TV. Maybe she went to sleep. That's what I usually do after a long cry. I put my key in to open my apartment, hoping that Brent isn't here. I open the door and hear the shower, well at least I don't have to face him. I try to close the door quietly hoping he wouldn't hear, as I shut the door. I hear the water stop. I try to run to my bedroom and before I get there, he has opened the bathroom door.

"Karma!"

My heart falls into my stomach. Is he mad at me? I sense a hint of aggression in his voice.

I look back at him sheepishly. His curly hair is still dripping wet from the shower along with the rest of his chiseled body. He just literally hopped out to yell at me. He turns fully toward me, holding the towel around his waist. Looking like he just stepped out of a Men's Health magazine. I feel my face fluster.

"Why are you avoiding me? This is only the third time I have seen you here in two weeks," he says.

I'm surprised. "Um, I'm not?"

He tucks in his towel and crosses his arms, leaning against the wall as he pursing his lips. His brows draw together with a face of disbelief.

"I- have just been busy," I lied. "Sorry I didn't know you missed me so much." I set my bag down in front of my bedroom door and I mimic him by crossing my arms with a smug look on my face.

He chuckles and rolls his eyes. "Well, are you busy right now?" he says.

I look around, and I noticed that he had cleaned up. The dishes were put away, and the counters were sparkling. And I finished my project already, so I guess I have nothing to do.

"No, why?" I say curiously. Why do I feel like he's flirting with me?

"I was just about to buy this new movie. It just came out and Ryan won't stop bugging me about watching it. So, why don't you join me, roomie?"

I just stare blankly at him for a second. Water clings to his skin, tracing the hard lines of his chest and abdomen before falling to the towel slung low on his hips. Steam curls around him, the scent of clean soap and something masculine fills the air. His muscles flex subtly as he runs his hand through his curly hair. He smirks, heat flickering in his honey light brown eyes, aware of exactly what he's doing. *He looks so good*. I feel myself pulse in between my legs.

"Okay," I say, trying to not smile. "I just need to change out of these clothes."

"Okay, I need to get dressed too anyway," he says as I close my door.

I put my back against the door and I giggle like a little schoolgirl. *What's happening? I'm overwhelmed. What am I going to wear?* I sniff my armpits and try to sniff in between my legs to see if I'm still fresh. It's a good thing I showered this morning instead of last night. I'll probably spray a little perfume to freshen up and a little more deodorant won't hurt.

Should I wear my sports shorts or would that look like I'm trying too hard? I feel my legs are a little stubby so no shorts. Should I just wear a full sweatsuit? *No, that will make me sweat, especially since I'm nervous and it won't do anything for my shape. I want to look hot but effortlessly.*

I settled on a fitted white tank top and some gray sweatpants. I let out a lungful of air and when I walk out, he is drying his beautiful, brown, curly hair with a towel.

As I walk in, I have to remind myself how he threatened to blackmail me, but he also carried me out of the bathroom that night and made sure I got home safe. I have to keep my guard up. When he gets his head out of the towel, he smiles big as soon as he sees me.

"Hey, I thought you probably changed your mind?" Is he insinuating that I took too long? I don't want him to think I was taking a long time trying to decide what to wear for *him*.

"Yeah, my mom called me up asking how to use the printer," I lied.

"Okay." He shrugs and puts on some band tee. "I already bought it. I just have to find the remote." He puts the rest of his clothes back in his suitcase, in the living room closet. He sits on the couch close to me with his legs spread. Well, he's not super close, but he is less than a foot from me. I'm at the corner of the couch with my legs to the left of me. He starts the movie. I feel him looking over at me, I look back at him nervously.

"Hey, I just wanted to say I'm sorry for trying to blackmail you like that. I was just desperate and was trying to justify what I was doing because you were doing it as well, which was so wrong of me, I'm so sorry. But I would never! I just want you to know that. I could leave if you want me to. I could just figure something out. I was angry and stressed, in a bad spot because the cops came that morning and said I can't sleep there anymore but I could find somewhere else to stay. Again, I'm sorry," he says abashedly.

I'm taken aback. I didn't expect him to apologize. "It's okay." I laugh. "I mean, I'm not innocent either. I appreciate your apology though, you're fine to stay however long. Honestly, I don't mind, I never enjoyed living alone anyway."

He smiles at me and I can see his eyes trace over my body. I get nervous, I can feel my stomach fluttering as I jump up from the couch.

"Do you want some popcorn?" I can tell my jump startled him.

"Um, sure," he says.

I don't even know if I have any popcorn. Or the last time I went grocery shopping? I'm searching in the pantry and all I found was gushers. Okay, this is embarrassing. I walk back over to the couch. Brent is looking back at me, waiting for my arrival.

"Okay, I have good news and bad news, which would you like first?" I ask.

"Bad news."

"Wow, what a pessimist. Um, there's a popcorn shortage. Yes, I know, disappointing. We should get a shipment next Thursday. But the good news is we're fully stocked with gushers," I say.

He lets out a slight chuckle. I can't tell if he's genuinely amused or just being polite. "That's the best news I've heard all year," he says in his New York accent.

I laugh as I go back in the kitchen to retrieve the box of gushers. We eat the entire thing while watching the movie. It was actually great. I didn't know Ryan had such good taste. It's a thriller movie. The jump scares surely make me jump with horror and Brent laughs. I'm guessing that's how we ended up getting so close on this couch. Now our knees are touching. The movie ends and we talk about how good it was, and make fun of the characters. As we are talking, the TV starts to auto-queue another movie, to some old Rom-Com.

We try to guess the title, as we didn't see it when it popped up. It has Candy Walters in it, as do most old Rom-Coms. We made a five-dollar bet on who could guess it first after about five guesses, I won. It was called "My Best Friend's Party." I know that because Candy Walters was my mom's favorite actress back then, we would watch all her movies over and over on VHS tapes. Those are my favorite memories from my childhood.

My mother always wanted to be just like her, especially in the movie, Pretty Lady. I celebrate my win by kicking my feet up, with my white crew socks on and clapping my hands as I laugh.

"Oh, wow, look at me! I won five dollars, I'm gonna be rich!" I say jokingly.

He smiles to himself as he goes to his backpack. "I

don't have any cash on me but I have this!" He pulls out this cat keychain with the tag on it, "Look, isn't it cute, it looks just like you!" he says with the key ring around his pointer finger looking pleased with himself.

Did he just call me cute? My cheeks grow red.

"I bought this yesterday, and I said to myself, this is a *dead ringer* for my new roommate," he says in a cheeky tone.

I snatched the key chain from him and read the tag on it. Ironically it says $5 on it as the price. This keychain cat is cute with brown eyes and dark brown hair to match mine. I do kind of look like this cat.

"Fair enough." I giggled.

He sits back down, now he's even closer to me than before. He takes the keychain from my hand slowly, in a way that his hands linger on mine.

"Where are your keys?"

I point to my room. "On my dresser,"

As he walks to my room. I open the camera app on my phone, check myself out, apply some lip gloss, fix my hair and check my teeth. *Oh no*, my mouth is blue from the candy, making me look like a toddler. It's kind of dark here. Maybe he won't notice. I hear him grab my keys and put the key chain on. He walks out of my room with a big smile on his face, proud of himself.

"Look at that," he says as he plops on the couch right beside me. His smile grows into laughter.

When he sits, I get a whiff of his scent. My God, he

smells good. I think it's his deodorant or aftershave. It just smells fresh and masculine in the best way. I feel another tingle in between my legs. Now we are just looking at each other.

"Um, thanks," I say as I take my keys from him.

"No, you won fair and square, brains and beauty," he says with a smirk on his face. I sense he is aware of his allure. I roll my eyes and push his shoulder playfully.

"Shut up," I say.

"What? You don't think so?" he says, grabbing the hand I pushed him with. I look down at his hand holding mine and snatch it away.

"No, It's not that. I know you're just trying to butter me up so I won't kick your cocky ass out of here," I say matter-of-factly.

He gasps dramatically with his hand on his chest, then says, "You think I'm trying to butter you up? Well, if I was, it's not to just stay here." he pauses. His light brown eyes search mine. "But is it working?" he says with a coy smile.

Is he talking about sex? *So corny.* I giggle.

I roll my eyes and push him again, but this time, he grabs my wrist—the same one I used to shove him—and pulls me closer.

Our faces are barely an inch apart. His gaze locks onto mine, then flickers down to my lips. A slow, knowing smile tugs at the corner of his mouth before he leans in, pressing his lips gently to mine.

His grip on my arm tightens slightly, sending a pulse of heat straight between my thighs. As we kiss, his hands slide down to my legs, fingers grazing my bare skin, and we fall into an effortless rhythm. Our tongues tease and explore, his hands roaming over me with a growing urgency. I wind my arms around his neck, pulling him closer as his lips travel down my jaw, then lower, his breath warm against my skin.

"Tell me when you want me to stop," he murmurs against my neck.

A soft groan escapes me as his fingers trail along my shoulder, pulling down the strap of my top and bra. His mouth moves lower, kissing a slow path to my chest, cupping my breast. I call his name in a breathy whisper that makes him pause. He looks up, searching my face.

After a moment, he nods, pressing a tender kiss to my lips before rolling onto his back against the couch. I glance down and see the unmistakable evidence of his arousal. A sudden surge of boldness has me reaching for him, my hand tracing over his hardness, stroking him through the fabric. But just as quickly, he catches my wrist, stopping me.

"We should wait," he whispers.

Something flickers in his expression—hesitation, reassurance? Is he trying to tell me that's not all he wants from me? *Or did he change his mind?*

"Yeah, you're right," I murmur, swallowing the lump in my throat. I shift back, suddenly self-conscious. "Um... I'm going to bed." I stand, feeling the heat of my own embarrassment creeping up my neck, unsure if I just dodge something-or if I lost something instead.

"Give me a goodnight kiss," he says as he pokes out his lips like a duck. I chuckle and peck him on the lips as I walk toward my bedroom door.

Brent yells, "Try not to dream about me!" From the couch.

I turn around and say, "You wish!" I close my door and I feel giddy like a schoolgirl. I've never really felt like this.

Wow, this is what all those movies are about, all these Rom-Coms. I'm like one of those girls now! I look at my phone and it buzzes a few more times. It was ironically vibrating on my lap while I was making out with Brent. It is Lucas and Athena. I almost forgot about the craziness of my life. I think now it's time to block him.

Now I'm sure I don't need this anymore. I feel guilty though, and what if Brent is just using me for sex and a place to stay? I can't be naïve. But he's so sweet. He got me this key chain, and he helped me out that night when Athena drugged me. I still can't believe that bitch. Maybe I'm being too nice. *Am I letting these people walk all over me? Or were the circumstances just unique? I'm not sure what to do.*

If I stop being friends with Athena and being whatever me and Brent are, I'll be alone. Is it worth it to be made to be a fool or to be sad and lonely like I have been my whole life? I'll just keep them at arm's length so they can't hurt me.

I'm having fun. I don't want to give that up yet. Yeah, I

mean Athena is a little crazy, but she's fun and I can gain a lot socially with her connections, money and charisma. I swear she could convince anyone to do whatever she wants. And Lucas? I'll figure something out later. I just don't have the heart or the confidence yet to let him go.

17

Diary entry- 7 years ago

PEOPLE KEEP MAKING comments about the way I look. The first person to do so was Dani. She asked me if I was dieting, if I got taller, or did something different with my hair. I shrugged and shook my head. I haven't been doing anything new.

Then she says "Whatever it is, it's working. You look good. You look exactly like Athena now." That's the common theme of everyone greeting me now that school started again. I'm a freshman now.

I have been thinking about a secret plan to save Dani. She's one of my closest friends now, besides Marie. Marie's parents never let her go out, even just to my house. I think they heard about my mom and her *problems.* Her parents are super strict.

My plan to help Dani is to ensure her mom receives additional medication before Dani gives her the usual dose at 6am. I researched which medications could potentially lead to an overdose and checked the ones in Dani's cabinet, noting that her mom takes several of them.

While Dani and my sister were asleep, I got up quietly and snuck into Dani's mother's room. I went through her bathroom and collected a few pills from each bottle. While searching through her drawers, I found all this paperwork, including her birth certificate, social security information, and even paperwork for life insurance. She had an application that she hadn't started. I glanced up at Dani's mother. She is still dead asleep breathing heavily.

I fill out the life insurance application, setting up a half-a-million-dollar life insurance policy with Dani as the main beneficiary. I will mail this off in the morning. So that she can afford the house, she won't have to move, and we could go shopping. I'm so excited.

It's time to put her mother out of her misery. She lives like a vegetable. The doctors don't even have any hope of her getting better, they just keep prescribing her more pills. She has chronic pain, low blood sugar, HIV and worsening vision every day, and she has blue hues in her eyes. She can't distinguish any of us girls apart.

The first day I gave her extra pills nothing happened. I had to do it for a week 'til she wouldn't wake up again. She choked on her own throw up. I don't know exactly what I was doing wrong. I'm not good at math. Afterward DHS took Dani. I don't know why, but she has the money to afford the house. Dani explained to us, it's because she is underage. She had to move far away. I haven't seen her for months. The police didn't even investigate her death, they just ruled it an accident.

Better news: I think Kyle likes me! He sits really close to me and he gave me his phone number that was just for me to send him the chemistry test answers but still he could have asked anyone else but no! He asked me!

18

Karma

THE NEXT MORNING, I wake up and I remember everything that happened last night, making me feel elated. Then I hear a slam of the door. That must have been Brent leaving. I look at the clock and see that I overslept. Oh no, I'm going to be late. Why didn't Brent wake me? I hurry and get dressed. Ugh, I didn't even shower last night. I have to go anyway. I grab some mints and hair brush, put deodorant and perfume in my bag, and run out to catch the next train to work.

While on the train, I finish getting ready. One thing I love about New York, people here mind their business. I applied deodorant on the train, pulled out a mirror to finish my hair and makeup, and nobody even looked at me. This place feels like home to me. I giggle to myself as I finish getting ready and, to my delight; I have lip gloss and mascara in my purse!

Now I look somewhat put together besides my

wrinkly shirt. I'll just tuck it in. Wow, I'm a resourceful genius. Look at me. Corporate girly, ready to take on the world. I walk in only two minutes late and no one is in the office. My panic sets in. When I call Ray, I hear him whisper, "Hello?"

"Where are you guys?" I whisper back. I don't know why.

"We are downstairs, the boss called in a meeting,"

"Okay, thanks, I'll be there in a minute." I hang up and run down the stairs. When I get there, people are just huddled together. I rush in and end up right behind Brent. His broad shoulders and the back of his head are instantly recognizable. I hit the back of his arm. He looks back at me with a frown and then his face lightens up as soon as he recognizes me.

"Hey," he says with a smile.

"Don't *'hey'* me. Why didn't you wake me up this morning? I overslept." I usually wake up an hour before I have to leave the house. He furrowed his thick brows with a sarcastic smile and tone.

"Sorry, I didn't know you needed a babysitter. I'll look into that for you though," he says as he turns around and the boss comes forth. I scuff and slap his forearm again playfully. He chuckles.

The chair of the company, Kathy Kelp, talks about the values of the company. Honestly, I'm not listening, just glad no one noticed I was late. I know Mr. Kelp would try to use that against me. She is talking about the strengths of individuals to further the company. Blah blah blah, I try to find Ray in the crowd. She then says that she regrets to inform us that we have lost a colleague, Josh Iverson, and to give thoughts and prayers to his family. Everyone gasps. I then try to remember where I heard that name.

Oh, that's Dani's boyfriend? Athena's friend or sister's friend from high school? What the hell? I scan the crowd for Athena. I don't see her. Then I look to my left and I see her walk up to me, hands on her mouth. She puts her hand on my shoulder and pulls me away.

"Karma," she says as she sniffles. "I can't believe this. See, I knew she was fucking evil. Told you I never liked her!" She shakes her head and makes crying noises. But as she looks up, I'm not seeing any tears.

"What are you talking about? Dani?" I ask.

"Yes! She—" Athena is still crying "You didn't hear her yelling at Josh a couple of days ago, because he went to the coffee shop with me after work to help me pitch my idea for the brand my section is working on. I heard her say that if he didn't stay away from me, then she would kill him! And- she did! I can't believe it, oh my God! Karma, oh, is this my fault?"

Now I can see that there were at least three tears dropped because of the streaks in her foundation and puddles in her eyes. Oh, I can't believe this.

"And you know what else? She conveniently didn't tell you that her sickly mom passed away in some freak accident!" Athena says matter-of-factly. "I knew there was something really wrong with her. I never liked her. She was such a bad influence on my sister getting her into trouble all the time! I think she must have had something to do with my sister's disappearance, too. This is too much of a coincidence!" She looks at me, almost as if she is waiting for my approval or agreement. At a loss for words, I just hug her.

"I'm so sorry. This is insane." I say, shocked. She cries some more. In the background I can hear everyone whisper to each other and some sniffles from the crowd. He's dead. I just talked to him a few days ago now he's gone?

Kathy speaks again, "So, in that respect we are going to close business today. Be ready tomorrow, though. We have a lot of work to do." Kathy Kelp announces as the crowd quiets down.

Athena looks up at me with puppy dog eyes. "Can you stay with me today? I don't want to be alone," she says with her head still on my shoulder. I look over at Brent. He's talking to some short girl with blonde hair. She looks cute. Are they flirting? I sigh and clench my jaw, feeling myself grow angry. I guess I won't be spending this time with Brent. It looks like he does not care enough to do so anyway.

"Yes," I say.

She perks up and says she'll call a car. She doesn't seem that upset anymore. Miraculously.

"They said they'll be here in ten minutes," she says in a cheery tone with a grip on my arm.

When we get back to her place, she insists we order

pizza and watch this soap opera about doctors. I told her I haven't seen it. She looks at me all wide-eyed.

"Oh, no. We have to watch it! I kind of envy you right now. I wish I could watch it for the first time again. You're going to love it!"

The show is pretty good. She gives me the background stories on the characters and opens up a bottle of wine for us to drink. It's one of those sweet red wine; Moscato.

We end up doing face masks and impressions, making fun of our bosses. Athena is fantastic at doing impressions. We get tipsy and start laughing at almost everything, but every time I drink with Athena, she never seems as drunk as I am. I end up passing out on her bed. When I wake up, I see Athena standing over me looking at her phone. I gasp, startled.

Athena looks down at me, puts her hands behind her back and says, "Girl, I'm sorry I was just putting you on your side. Just in case you throw up, so you don't choke." She pats my shoulder. "Go back to bed."

I fall asleep almost immediately.

Once I wake up, I jolt up trying to find a clock. I almost forgot where I was, and that it was the weekend. I look at the clock and it's 10:30, Sunday. Oh, thank God I put my hand on my chest, relieved. I hear Athena in the kitchen. Sounds like she's cooking breakfast. I search the bed for my phone and I find it under the bed at five percent. My head throbbing, I hold the side of my head and stubble into the kitchen.

"Hey, sleepy head! I'm making omelets. Do you want one?" she says in an upbeat tone.

How is she not hungover? Maybe she's used to drinking. I can't remember the last time I drank before I got to New York. She is a kind of party girl. It'll probably take a lot for her to get drunk. Let alone be hungover. Then I think about last night. I'm surprised Athena has so much enthusiasm after everything that just happened. She seemed so distraught yesterday. Maybe this is a part of her coping mechanisms. Deflecting and distracting. I couldn't imagine losing a sister. Or having a coworker, I know get murdered by a childhood friend.

Especially since she said that she thinks it could be her fault. I feel so bad for her. We saw last night that Dani got arrested on the news. The new reporter said that Dani, Danielle Ortiz says she's innocent but the police received an anonymous tip with compelling evidence, Athena didn't say she was the one to give the tip, but I know she did.

She's handling this well, she's being so strong. I smile at her, trying to match her energy even though I have none. I see a notification pop up on my phone. Hoping it's Brent, I get a little excited. Is he not even worried that I didn't come home? Ugh. The notification was from Lucas. I swipe it up as soon as it pops up. I can't have Athena see me messaging him. Athena has been rambling about how her dad taught her to make the best omelets, and how he would say "omelets" funny because of his accent or something.

"Karma? What do you think?"

I have dazed off thinking about all the drama going on at work and Brent. "Sorry, I'm a little hung over." I laugh.

"A party! Shouldn't we throw a party in remembrance of Josh? He would want his life to be celebrated and not mourned, don't you think?" she says.

I kind of looked at her blankly. *Celebrated?* Someone murdered him. She looks so excited about it, I just nod.

"Yeah. I mean, I didn't know him but that sounds... Thoughtful." I say.

"That's what I'm saying! Okay, yay I think it is going to be so fun!" she said, handing me an omelet.

As I eat, she tells me more about where we should host the party, that she will email everyone from Introspection to come. And that we should do it on the beach because Josh loved the beach. I don't know how she knows him so well. We have only been at Introspection for a few weeks. I don't bother to ask. My stomach starts to turn.

"Well, I need to run some errands to prepare everything," she said, looking at me.

"I'm going to go back to my apartment and probably just get some Gatorade and take a nap," I say.

As I grab my phone and the rest of my stuff. She nods quickly and goes to open the door for me. Like she's rushing me out.

"Oh, okay, I'll see you later," I say as I walk out the door. She does a quick smile and shuts the door in my face. That was odd. It seems like she just got upset with me. Is it because I wasn't paying enough attention to her story? I think it's maybe because a lot is going on right now.

I walk into my apartment, and I see Brent on the couch. "Hey," he says nonchalantly to me.

I doubted he would even be here. This makes me regret not looking in the mirror before I left Athena's. I mean, she didn't even give me a chance to do anything, just rushing me out like that. I try to brush my hands against my curly hair to fix my bedhead.

"Hey," I say back and just rush toward my bedroom.

"Hey, you want to watch TV or something?" he yells out to me.

I look back, my hand already on my door. "Yeah, um, I just need to shower and stuff first," I say.

"You and Athena, went out last night? I saw y'all leave together," he says.

Wow, he noticed we had left together? He must have been looking for me and said nothing, seeing that Athena was distraught. Despite his care, I can't help but feel angry when I remember seeing him talking to that girl. I turn away and remark,

"Oh, I'm surprised you noticed us. I thought you were too busy chatting with that blondie."

He laughs. "What? Oh yeah, she was asking me how to get back to the parking garage. I had no clue who she was. Hmmm, are you jealous?" He says as he stands walking toward me as if he's challenging me.

"No," I say, crossing my arms. I can tell he's not being persuaded.

He has a devilish grin on his face as he keeps slowly walking closer to me.

"Jealousy looks good on you," he says as his eyes trace my body. I'm wearing some tiny blue sleep shorts Athena let me borrow and a tight black tank top with no bra.

"You really have such a nice body. So sexy," he says under his breath, but loud enough for me to hear.

As his eyes make it up to mine, he steps closer, puts his hand on my waist, then the small of my back as he kisses me. A tingle runs down my back, then in between my legs. I push him away quickly and step back.

"Sorry, I just need to shower and brush my teeth and stuff," I laugh awkwardly.

He shrugs. "You smell fine to me."

I think he's just horny, but I'm not gonna hook up with him without a shower. That would only make me ten times more self-conscious than I already am. I giggle to myself. "Thanks, but no I'm going to shower."

"Okay, well I have to go to work in a little."

"Okay, um Athena's throwing a party tonight you should come if you're not still working!"

"I'll see," he says, walking back to the couch to gather his stuff.

"All right, I'll see you later," I close my door. Then I hear the living room door shut.

Why is he in such a rush now that we aren't gonna hook up? Is he going to see another girl or is he really working? I open my bedroom door and go to the living room to look at the couch and in the closet to see if he took his work stuff, he did. Hm, maybe he's honest. I think I'm being paranoid. *Why can't I believe a boy actually likes me?* Maybe because it never really happens, but men lie and they are guilty until proven innocent. I have to make sure I'm not letting my walls down. But I definitely want to have fun with him. He's so sexy, and he thinks I'm sexy!

When I check the time, I'm surprised to see it is already noon. I'm going to wash and deep condition my hair, skin care, and everything! Me and Brent are going to have sex tonight, hopefully! I'm getting excited just thinking about it. Tonight's gonna be so fun! I also need to find something to wear tonight! I wonder if Athena will let me borrow something of hers.

19

Diary entry- 6 years ago

AFTER DANI LEFT, my sister and I started hanging out more. Lately, many people say they can't tell us apart. I get called Athena so much. It's weird, but I kind of like it. People are nicer to me and give me more attention because they think I'm her. I sometimes forget how many friends she has.

I've even started wearing her clothes, her skirts, short shorts, and colorful outfits. So, I can feel girly and pretty. Normally, I stick to wearing dark colors, just trying to blend in. Now I have let my hair grow out. My auburn hair is down my back. It frames my face a lot better, like Athena's. So, I can see why people think we look so much alike.

Plus, I've filled out! I finally have boobs and hips! Sometimes Athena yells at me about stealing her clothes and I just lie and say all of mine are dirty or don't fit. She knows mom won't buy me an entire new wardrobe.

Now me and Athena are the same size and about the same height. I used to be two sizes bigger. Guess I'm just what they call a late bloomer. My mom says I lost my baby weight.

Yesterday, Dani came to visit since spring break just started. When Athena and I got into the truck with her and her boyfriend, Dani looked at us in the backseat like she'd seen a ghost. "What the fuck you guys look like Siamese twins!" Athena rolled her eyes and called me a copycat. I hit her arm and said my clothes don't fit anymore. She rolls her eyes at me, again.

The talent show auditions are next week! I'm so excited! I think I'm going to sing a song from one of my favorite movies.

20

Karma

As I'm washing my face, I hear my phone ding repeatedly. After rinsing my face off and wiping my hands, I look at my phone. I see a bunch of Instagram messages saying I forgot my password, a password reset link was sent to my email, and that someone is logging into my account from an unknown phone. My heart pounds. *Oh no.*

I try to go into my email and click on the link. It says it expired, and I can't get in. Then I try to go to Instagram and select that I forgot my password, it tells me it sent to an email I don't recognize. I look into all my notifications I got previously. There are multiple messages from Lucas right before. What's going on? The unrecognized phone login was from last night, and now I just got logged out. I'm freaking out. Maybe it's just some bot.

I've heard about those. It has happened to my friends before, but that's when I woke up and saw Athena hovering over me with a phone. Was that my phone? No, the case was black. My case is sparkling red. Maybe that's why my ringer is on, because she switched the case. No, why would she do that? She wouldn't. I'm probably just being paranoid. I need to stop. Maybe this was just a blessing in disguise. I no longer need that account. I no longer need Lucas.

I'm okay. Everything's okay, I say to myself in the mirror. Taking a few deep breaths and then turning my phone on silent. I try to not think about it and finish getting ready. Tears are welling up in my eyes. I'm not completely sure why. Maybe saying goodbye. Are they guilty or happy tears? So many emotions go through me as I finish getting ready. Then I call Athena. She doesn't answer. I wonder what she's doing. I'm trying to find an outfit, but I'm not finding anything I really like. I wonder what everyone else will be wearing. I hesitate to call Athena again, afraid of coming off weird. We spent all day together last night, so I guess that wouldn't be weird. I see my phone ring and it's Athena. "Hey!"

"Hi," she says unenthusiastically.

"What are you doing?"

"I'm at the house, setting up with Kendall and Jada, the girls from Introspection. Why?" says Athena. I feel my stomach turn with jealousy and sadness. Why didn't she invite me to help?

"Uh, nothing. I was just going to see what you were wearing to the party because I can't find anything," I say.

"Girl, do you not have your own clothes?" She laughs.

"Of course, I just don't know the vibe." I say my shyness with embarrassment.

"Slutty, um, short black dress." Athena declares. I hear people's voices in the background as she yells, "I gotta go. I'm busy. Hurry though. I'll text you the address." She hangs up.

I look at the clock. It's already 8:30 p.m. I picked out this jean mini skirt, a white tube top, and my white Nike sneakers. I sit on the edge of my bed till she texts me the address forty-five minutes later.

I call a taxi and I get there around ten. It seems like everyone is here already, many people I don't recognize. It's this big beach house on a hill, in the Hamptons. Very modern style with its hardwood floors, large windows and marble black countertops, sleek leather brown furniture, tall ceilings, a huge balcony, with a beautiful view over the water. It looks so expensive, maybe one of those men Athena keeps talking to bought it.

I walk through the crowd, trying to look for someone I know. Making my way into the kitchen because I'm uncomfortable. I'll buy myself some time and get a drink. As soon as I got here, I texted Athena. I haven't gotten a response yet. I text her again and tell her I'm in the kitchen. A few minutes later, I see Athena walk into the kitchen with a big smile on her face, red lips and a blunt in between her teeth. She's wearing a little black spaghetti dress that hugs her slim hourglass body, thigh-high boots, with her hair blown out. She looks so good, effortlessly it seems.

"Glad you made it!" she says as she hugs me. Now that I'm close to her. I can see that her eyes are bloodshot, under her long eyelashes. Which only makes her look more carefree and pretty.

"I'm happy I found the place, which it seems like everyone else did, practically the entire company?" I laugh as I take a sip of my drink.

She looks around, shrugs, and says, "I don't know most of these people," smiling as she blows smoke from her blunt in my direction. As her phone dings she turns away from me. Then looks back at me with a mischievous grin.

"What?" I ask.

"Nothing!" she says theatrically. "I'm just happy you're here." She grabs my shoulders. Then I see her looking in the crowd waving her hands over to someone.

I quickly finish my drink, knowing I'm going to need to be social. I'm in need of some liquid courage. So, I go back to the fridge and grab another beer. Open it and turn around and I see *him*. It's him. It's Lucas. I freeze. Athena is just smiling, looking back and forth at us.

She knows.

This evil bitch. Why would she do this? I'm horrified by my worst nightmare. I thought I could just leave this behind. My eyes fill with water.

"This is—" Athena says as I run out of the kitchen toward the hallway crying, trying to find somewhere to hide.

When I go into the first door I see, I find people smoking. I close it and go into the furthest room, guessing it is the master bedroom because it has its own bathroom. I run into the bathroom and lock the door. So humiliated, I sit on the toilet and cry. This means she was looking through my phone. She changed my phone case and was looking over me to make sure I didn't wake up? She must have remembered my passcode from my phone and logged in and invited him here.

Why would she do that? I thought she was my friend. Fucking bitch. She has ruined everything. I wonder if she told him already. She's going to tell everybody I'm a psycho freak and I'm going to have to move back home. I'm so stupid. As I cry uncontrollably and struggle to breathe, I hit myself with my hands. I am hyperventilating, I think I'm having a panic attack.

Then I hear someone walk into the bedroom. I put my hands over my mouth, as two people come in and sit on the bed. I hear a girl giggling, followed by them making out and moaning. *Oh no I can't stay here any longer.* I look in the mirror and try to clean myself up. My mascara has smeared all over my face, and there are streaks in my foundation. I wipe my face hard to get rid of the makeup, leaving my face raw and red. I unlock the bathroom window and quietly jump out and walk around the house to the front so I can get to the street and call a cab home.

I feel so hopeless. There is no way out of this. Oh my gosh when Brent finds out, he's going to think I'm some insecure crazy bitch and never talk to me again. I put my head in my hands and keep walking on around the house.

Then I see Lucas. He's smoking a cigarette. We catch each other's eyes at the same time. Fuck. I have to face him. A part of me always wanted to. I owe him that. Running away is no longer an option for me. I smile at him. He smiles back with a concerned look on his face.

"Are you okay?" He asks. He's probably wondering why I ran away like that.

"Oh yeah, sorry I just got sick, too much beer probably." I try to laugh it off. He probably thinks I'm strange. Wait until he finds out.

"Oh okay. Um, Athena said you would know where Anastasia was?"

I look down while playing with my fingers. Okay, now is the time. I have to just do it. What's the worst that could happen? *Maybe he'll see that all I lied about was a picture.*

"Ya about that—" I say.

"Oh, I recognize you!" My stomach drops again. Maybe he's always known?

"You used to work at Red Robin as a hostess for like two weeks. I see why you quit though; I hated that place too." He laughs.

Well, at least I know that's why he was always angry and it wasn't just me. That makes what I'm about to say even worse. I start to shake and sweat.

"Oh, yeah, um, I just wanted to tell you I'm sorry. But everything I said was true, and I love you and," I say timidly.

He steps back. "What are you talking about?" He's looking at me like I have three heads. I take a deep breath and I can feel myself crying again.

"I'm Anastasia. I have been this whole time, but I knew it was wrong. But I just really liked you. Believe me, I tried to stop! I didn't invite you here. Athena made some sick joke! I would never do that to you! I'm so sorry, but everything I said was the truth I swear! I never wanted this to happen!" I say in one breath, gasping, still shaking.

He shakes his head. "No, you're not. I have had *sex* with Anastasia. I know you're not her," he says.

I can tell now he's questioning everything. He's frowning and looking at me and back ahead at the water.

"There's no way, what the fuck! What is wrong with you?" he says as his jaw clenched and tightened mouth.

"I'm not lying. I wish I was," I say in a weak and tremulous whisper.

"Prove it."

"I don't have the account anymore. I told you she hacked it," I whisper, trying not to anger him anymore than I already have.

"Do you know about Anthony?" he says I can tell he's hoping I don't.

"Yeah."

"No, tell me then," he says.

"He passed."

"How?" His face is red and eyes are wide and glossy.

"Car accident," I say with my head down.

He puts his hand on his head, pacing back and forth

"There's no fucking way no f—" he says under his breath. I feel scared, but I know he won't hurt me. He's a sweet guy, and he loves me. I come toward him and try to console him, with my arm out.

"Don't touch me," he says as he steps back. He has tears in his eyes, a vein poking out his forehead, and his nostrils flared. He is livid.

"I'm sorry," I say as I hold my hands up, backing away.

"I had sex with Anastasia. She was wearing a mask for that party, but her hair and accent I..." he says.

"It was a wig. I'm sorry I just wanted to be close to you, because I love you, Lucas, you have to know that," I say in Anastasia's Australian accent.

His eyes grow wide. Now he's fully convinced I can tell.

"You disgusting freak, what the—what is wrong with you? Love what—? I don't fucking know you! You're crazy!"

"But you do, Lucas. You do, please don't do this. I'm sorry I tried to stop what I did! I didn't want to hurt you anymore because I love you, I love—" I say, tears streaming down my face, holding my arms out, my hands trembling trying to plead with him.

"Shut up shut up!" he yells, lunging toward me as he grabs my throat. Pushing me backwards, making us fall, but he doesn't loosen his grip. I feel like this is it.

This is how I die. When we stop rolling, I try to regain my balance, but he gets back on top of me, choking me. I black out.

21

Diary entry 6 years ago

I HATE ATHENA. Fucking bitch. She stole my song for the talent show by making sure she auditioned before me. I was so shocked when they called my name, I just froze and left. Humiliated. This was my thing. I know she taught me how to sing, but that was when we were in the children's choir at church. We don't even go to church anymore. I don't even know how she knew I would have sung that song.

Another thing I told her, I had a crush on Kyle, she said he was cute, and now she talks to him every day. Now they are basically dating. Why is she doing this? I thought we were becoming friends. If she wants to make me her enemy, I'll play that role. SHE WILL TAKE NOTHING ELSE FROM ME. I don't know what I'm going to do, but I'm going to get my way. I just need to find out something so she can't make the show.

And for Kyle I never really had the courage to tell him I like him, but everything would be so much easier if he thought I was Athena. I could skip all the awkward stuff. Like trying to gauge his feelings and flirt. It would already be established.

22

Karma

I WAKE up to Athena slapping me in the face. "Get up! Get up! Fuck!" she says.

I hold my face, hot from the slap, and then I touch my neck. The first thing I remember is him choking me. I was sure he was going to kill me. I'm disoriented, all I hear is the music echoing from the party still going on and Athena yelling at me.

"Get up and help me!" When I get up my body hurts. "We need to get him in the water and maybe throw some rocks on him," she grunts, losing her breath. "Fuck, he's too big!" She leans over to catch her breath.

Still trying to understand what's going on, I look at Lucas. Lucas is dead? He is just laying here, lifeless with a wound on the side of his head where his temple is. There is a lot of blood and there is also blood on a rock that's the size of my hand, next to me. I keep looking at everything back and forth.

"Athena w—what happened?" I say hysterically.

"What do you think happened? He was choking you the fuck out because you used fake pictures to talk to him for years, borderline raped him, and I saved your life. That's what happened. Now come over here and help me!" I nod and grab his foot while Athena takes the other, and we drag him into the water.

We end up soaking wet, pulling him into the water and placing some heavy rocks on top of his body so his body won't float up. It's a good thing that when Lucas and I rolled down the steep hill, we rolled to the shore where there were plenty of rocks.

As we walk back up the hill, all I'm thinking is how much of our messages did she read, or did she just over-hear us? The music was so loud, and we weren't that close to the house. She hacked into my account. That's how she invited him here.

Why am I following her? She's not my friend; she caused all of this.

I stop walking. But she did save me. I'm guessing she hit him from behind with that rock. Why did she say that I borderline raped him? Was it to make it seem that I wasn't innocent, or is she afraid that I will report her? Well, I can't now because I helped her cover it up and I'm holding the rock. She ensured I would help her. Now I have no way out of this. My life is ruined. Athena looks back and notices I stopped following her. We lock eyes.

"Why the fuck did you do this to me? What have I ever done to you?" I yell.

She comes toward me with a melancholy look, shaking her head. "No, no, Karma, I was trying to help you. When I was younger, I was just like you. I knew you just needed a little push. You know, you honestly do follow me around like a lost puppy. You're just so insecure and sheltered. I sensed something was off about you too. So, once I found out I wasn't that surprised.

He's not even all that. Sure, I mean he's cute. Well, he was, but you're pretty! I thought if you met him in a party setting, with a cute outfit on, you guys would hit it off. But you fucked it up, and he was a psycho, anyway. Who puts their hands on a girl like that? I mean I get why he was mad, but now he's dead. So, we have to get the fuck out of here." She turns around, grabbing my arm.

Why is she acting so flippant about this? We could go to prison forever, and a boy just died. Lucas is dead. He was someone I loved. I feel like I want to cry, but nothing is coming out. I'm numb, I think I'm in shock. *What should I do?* The party is still going on. I can see people are still dancing around, laughing, drinking, and having fun. I don't even know what time it is. Athena's looking for the room she put her bags in. She finds it and climbs in the window.

"I'm so glad I brought extra clothes," she says as she throws me something to wear and changes herself.

After I change, I just stand there in shock. She takes all the clothes, the rock and zips in the suitcase and we leave out the back. We make sure no one sees us. Then

Jada walks out and we make eye contact. I jump. Which makes Jada jump, and she giggles. "Are you good?"

"She just had a little too much to drink, so we're going home," Athena says.

Jada sighs in relief. "Great, I'm ready to go. This guy would not leave me alone and I have been looking all over for you two. Where were you guys?"

"Um, I was helping her out. She started throwing up really bad, yeah."

"Aww, Karma, okay hope you feel better. We should get some pho in the morning; it's the best hangover food!" Jada says to me.

"Yeah," I say, trying to sound calm.

"Let me go grab my purse and I'll be ready to go!" Jada says as she runs in. Me and Athena just look at each other. Jada comes back quickly; we leave and call a taxi. I keep looking over my shoulder. I feel like someone might have seen us. There were so many people here.

Athena and Jada are just talking back and forth like nothing happened. I keep checking my phone and the news, frantically. Should I call the cops? Athena was basically acting in self-defense for me. What do they call that? Um, yeah defense of others, yes. It can work. I need his phone, though. Fuck, we left his phone. Well, he doesn't have my number. But he has the address to the party. Well, I didn't rent the house. But if I talk to the cops, Athena will rat me out. She's the reason all this happened, anyway. And she says she is trying to help me? Please, and I don't follow her like a puppy. I thought we were getting close. See, I knew this was too good to be true.

The taxi stops to let Jada out, she says she's going to see her ex. We wish her good luck. She holds out her tongue and winks. Now it's just me and Athena, once we get out, we walk together. I hesitate. I don't want anyone to overhear us. Walking through the busy streets, it's still busy way past midnight. I whisper to her, "His phone. We need to get his phone."

"I have it." I feel a slight sense of relief. I'm also bewildered. How is she always two steps ahead of me?

"I got it while you were unconscious. It's dead," she says.

"Okay, so we need to charge it, but not at our place. Maybe a gas station?" I say. Athena nods. We buy a charger at the gas station and decide to sit in McDonald's while the phone charges. Athena gets a Big Mac meal. How can she even eat right now?

We get his phone on. But it's locked. "What would his passcode be?"

I shrug. "Come on, you were basically dating this boy for years," Athena says, rolling her eyes. "What's his birthday? Mom's birthday?"

"Lucas's birthday is June 5. Moms I don't know." She tries 0605. It doesn't work.

"I'll look at his Facebook for his moms," I say.

We try his mom's, his brother's and everyone's. We end up locking the phone for five minutes. Athena's just looking at me like I'm an idiot, then looks away and drinks her sprite. I feel embarrassed again. I can't believe she found out. My stomach turns. But if we do everything right, it will be okay.

"You won't tell anyone, right?" I whisper with my head down.

"No. I won't tell anyone. Only if you tell me why you did it," she says tauntingly.

I feel my cheeks grow red. She has no right to question me.

"Why were you looking through my phone? Using fake pictures online isn't a crime, but killing someone is," I say.

"But who would believe I did that? Especially, if they find out you were using fake pictures to fuck him. You invited him over to the house, hoping the physical attraction and admiration would be requited. When it wasn't, you got angry and killed him, because he threatened to expose you to your new friends and you couldn't let that happen, could you? So, why did you do it? I want a play-by-play," she says with a grin of amusement.

I tell her a short story. "I saw him on a dating app and I thought he was so cute, and his bio was funny. I felt like I knew we would get along and everything but we didn't match. So, I created another one using this girl's picture that was popular on Tumblr and we matched. Then the rest is history," I explain.

"Okay, but how did you pull off having sex with him?" Her eyes get wide. I can tell she is eager to find out. I paused. I don't want to tell her. That's too personal.

"Oh. I know! I know the passcode." I grab the phone and the five minutes are over. Thank God. I type in 0106. The passcode was his friend's birthday, the one that passed. We get in, delete all of Athena's messages, unfollow her on Instagram and my fake Anastasia account.

"Why did you hack my account?" I ask.

"I didn't." She looks at me like I'm dumb.

"Then who did Athena? Okay, how did you even invite him then?" I ask.

"You literally just watched me unfollow myself weirdo, that's how I invited him. I said I was a friend of Anastasia's and that I'm throwing a party, and that you— well Anastasia wanted me to send him all the details. That's how."

I can't tell if she's lying or not. Who else would hack my account? Whatever, it doesn't matter now. It's deleted. We then take the SIM card out of his phone, step on it outside and then throw his phone into traffic. I let out a deep breath. Now I can relax a little.

"What are we going to do with the suitcase?" I ask her.

"I'll take care of it, trust me."

"What are you going to throw it somewhere?"

"No, I'm going to get someone to take it far away and eradicate it. Okay," she says to me like I'm a toddler.

We walk back toward our apartment. She walks ahead of me, like ten feet ahead of me, looking at her phone. I just think about how I got myself into this.

When I make it back, Brent's on the couch waiting for me.

"Hey, sorry I missed the party. How was it?" he says.

I pull my face into a smile. "It was really exhausting. I need to shower," I say.

"Yeah, I can tell. You look exhausted," Brent says, he sounds a little disappointed. Like he'd hoped we were gonna hang out.

I get in the shower and cry some more. When I get out, I notice the marks on my neck. Why am I sad he's dead? He literally tried to kill me? Well, that's because of what I did to him.

There are one hundred plus episodes of Catfish, and I'm sure none of them end in attempted murder. His response was insane, Athena's right. I was just trying to let him know I love him and that my feelings were genuine. Then he attacked me. I always knew he had a temper, but I never thought he'd be like that to me.

Walking to my bedroom, carrying my clothes. I can't help but feel like I'm responsible for his death, though. Athena saved me. I return to my bedroom wrapped in a towel, lay on my bed, and fall asleep immediately.

23

Diary entry 5.75 years ago

I GOT to perform at the show. It was really fun. People started calling me Athena, again. Well, I guess that was partially my fault because I didn't tell people I was replacing her.

After the show was over, Athena's boyfriend, Kyle, was so proud of me. He hugged me real tight and kissed me! I don't feel bad about that. I liked him and Athena just started dating him to one-up me. It's not the first time me and Kyle hooked up; well, made out and stuff. I think he knows but I'm not sure. I haven't asked. After the show, we went to his house and had sex. It was just like what I had imagined. I knew he would be amazing. I don't know what I'm going to do about Athena.

I might have given her too much. I'm home now and she still won't wake up. Yesterday morning, I crushed the pills up and put them in her coffee. It's now eight o'clock in the morning, and Kyle just dropped me off. I even put my finger under her nose—I think she's breathing. She should wake up soon.

The pills are antidepressants I found in my mom's cabinet—the ones that make her sleepy. So, they should be safe. Still, I feel like I don't have a lot of time left to do what I need to do. I search for her phone and find it under her pillow. I go through all her messages on her little Sidekick.

First, I deleted the messages from Kyle talking about last night. Then out of curiosity, I check to see if she's been talking shit about me. To my surprise, she hasn't.

I move on to her pictures. It's just some of her with friends and a few of our dog, Skip. Nothing incriminating.

Now I'm bored. I put her body in a sleep-like position, and head to school. At school, people keep asking, "Where's your sister?"

I can tell they don't know which one I am, so I say, "Oh, Serena's not feeling well." They nod and talk about class or whatever.

I had to hold my amusement all day. People called me Athena over and over. I even went to her classes, which was hilarious—until I overheard what other people thought about me. They spoke openly thinking I was her. They laugh about how embarrassing I am because I froze at the audition, how I was shy, chubby, and now I'm trying to act 'cool'. I just stared at them, seething, and tried to come up with insults to hurl at them. Nothing clever came to mind.

I got home around five after hanging out with Kyle again.

Once I got back, Athena hadn't moved. Panic started to creep in. I tapped her shoulder and then shook her, hard. Still nothing. I turn her onto her back. Her face is pale, almost white, with white foam-like substance coming out her mouth. My heart starts racing. I slapped her face, lightly at first, then harder trying to wake her. No response.

I panic. What could I tell my mom? The police? I think she's dead. She can't be dead. There is no way. But why hasn't she moved in over twelve hours? Then an idea hit me. I could bring Mom's bottle in her room, leave it in her bed, and say she overdosed herself. Yes, that could work!

I run to my mom's room and everything moved. She cleaned? She hasn't cleaned in weeks. Then I see her in the kitchen doing the dishes. She says she has a guy coming over tonight and that me and my sister should go to Dani's tonight. That's why she's cleaning.

I go back upstairs and slap Athena around a little more. Nothing.

I sit up and wait till about 4 a.m. and I wrap Athena up in her covers and drag her to my mom's car. It feels like someone might have seen me. I ignore that thought, drive two towns over, and drop her body by the garbage, at a truck stop gas station.

After calling the cops on her phone, I throw it in the garbage. Somebody might find her eventually and they will be her problem. I fill up the gas tank and drive home. And get ready for school that day again as Athena. I am Athena now. Athena with a scholarship, a boyfriend and best friends with Dani. I win.

24

Karma

THE FEELING OF A SUNDAY MORNING, free from work, brings initial happiness, but a wave of anxiety hits my stomach as I remember last night. I feel sick. I look at my phone with no texts. Then I check the news and no one has found him. Drawing in a deep breath, I cry again on my pillow. He tried to kill me. He tried to kill me. I keep telling myself. But this guilt is eating at me. I stare at the ceiling for hours. I haven't left my bed yet and it's two p.m.

Then Brent knocks on my door. "Hey, Karma?"

"Yes?" I say my voice caught in my throat. He probably thinks I'm a lazy loser. With nothing else better to do.

The silence stretched as he said. "Are you okay?" His voice was concerned.

"Ya, why do you say that?" I say, trying to sound chipper, knowing exactly why he asks that.

"You haven't left your room yet. I was wondering if you were hungry? I could order some pizza?" he suggests.

My stomach growls at the thought of pizza. I feel like I don't deserve this. I can't imagine what he would say or how he would treat me if he found out. Maybe I should just enjoy this while it lasts. Enjoy him. The thought of being with him makes me smile. I feel a sudden burst of energy.

"Finally! I thought you'd never ask!" I say. Getting out of bed naked, I throw on black shorts without underwear, and a pink zip-up jacket without a bra. I finger-comb my long curly hair and zip my jacket a little low, just enough to show a hint of cleavage. I open the door and Brent is standing there in a fitted black tee shirt, black 5-inch seam shorts that show off his muscular legs, and thigh tattoo. He's incredibly attractive. He's looking at me with his infectious grin that sets the tone. *He likes me.*

"Hey!" I say with my head down, suddenly remembering I haven't brushed my teeth yet.

"Hey glad you're alive," he says.

"Yeah, last night. Um, it was a long night."

"I bet," he says. He has no idea.

"I'm going to go to the bathroom then we can order that pizza."

I walk into the bathroom. *Glad you're alive?* Does he know? What if he came to the house and saw what happened and then left? *Glad you're alive, why would he say that?* It's just a joke; he said that because I have been in my room all day. If he knew, he would have looked at me completely differently. He doesn't know. I need to just block that out of my mind for right now, at least.

I brush my teeth while avoiding the mirror. I can't even look at myself. I just look down at my outfit, feeling silly. It's not as sexy as I'd imagined. After I finish brushing my teeth, I walk out with my tail between my legs.

"I was thinking of a Big Mama's Pizza. It has great reviews and is next door," he says,

"That sounds good. Do you like jalapeños and chicken as the toppings?"

He nods, puts in the order and sits down on the couch. I do the same. We sat close.

"Was the party fun?" he asked.

"No, it sucked. I should have just stayed here. I wish I had stayed here. It's honestly not even worth talking about." I chuckle, desperately trying to change the subject.

"How was work yesterday?"

"It was cool. I probably stacked a thousand bricks, super fun." His voice is heavy with sarcasm.

Moments later we hear a ring at the door. I jumped up.

"That was fast!" As I go to the door, I look through the peephole first. I'm not sure why, but something is telling me to. Maybe it's the paranoia. I gasp at the peephole. I see it's Athena. She can't know Brent lives here.

"It's Athena," I whisper.

He raises his eyebrows. "What do you want me to do?"

I shake my head and put my finger on my lips, signaling to him to be quiet. I can't handle this right now. I don't even want to think about what happened last night, let alone her. But she did save my life.

Whatever it is, it can wait or she'll figure it out. One thing I have learned about Athena is she is resourceful. I sit back down, and wait for her to leave. But I can't stop thinking about it. What if it was important? What if they found the body, and she wanted to come up with a plan? But can I even trust her? My mind races as Brent tells me about another movie. I interrupted him.

"Sorry, I'm just going to call her and make sure she doesn't need anything." I rush toward my room and scour my bed looking for my phone. I can't find it. Then I look under my bed, throwing my shoes and clothes all over the room and there it is. I only have three percent battery on my phone, but it'll do. When I call Athena. It goes straight to voicemail. I call again and again with no answer. Now I'm getting worried. Hopefully, nothing has happened to her. What if they've already taken her into custody, or she's gone to the police and blamed me for everything? I pace in my bedroom. Then I get a call from Athena.

"Hello? Is everything all right, what's going on?" I say frantically, trying to keep my voice down.

"Nothing. Are you alone?" she asks.

"Yes," I lied.

"You liar. I heard a man in there, you whore. You were out here two-timing Ol' boys, huh?" She chuckles. "I didn't expect that from you. I'm impressed, anyways I was just bored and wanted to grab lunch. Oh, and I wanted to tell you everything's cleaned. You're welcome, bye," she says as she hangs up the phone.

I exhale a breath, that I feel like I have been holding for ten mins. *Okay, I smile, everything's All right, it's done.* I promise myself not to think about it for the rest of the day, and pretend like it never happened. I walk back out and there is another ring at the door. This time it's the pizza. I grab it from the man and smile at Brent.

"Okay, what was that movie you wanted to watch?" I say as I go to grab some plates.

"It's a show about a school teacher whose brother-in-law works for the DEA. He runs into one of his prior students who makes meth during a raid, after he's diagnosed with cancer, he teams up with his prior student to produce and sell meth!" he says in an excited tone.

"That sounds good. Put it on!" I replied. We watched a few episodes, chatting during the commercials.

He shares that he ended up living in his car after discovering his girlfriend, Bianca, of a year was cheating on him with her coworker. Without saying anything, he packed his things and left. *Who would cheat on him?* I told him about how my mom went to jail for stealing from famous people. He laughs and calls it a victimless crime, like when he started making fake IDs in college for some extra cash. I laughed too; he has a point.

I explain how my mom was in and out of jail, so I had to live with my grandparents on and off again. He tells me his parents divorced when he was a baby. He was raised by his mom as a single mother. He shares how excited he is to be here, fulfilling his dreams, and I tell him I feel the same way.

We usually only strike up conversations during commercials. But once this Lysol commercial plays, we lock eyes and I feel a flutter in my stomach and a pulse between my legs. He looks down at my lips, then back to my eyes, parts his mouth and kisses me softly, placing his hand on my thigh. I kiss him back using my tongue. I hear him groan, which excites me even more.

I climb on his lap and unzip my jacket, revealing my breasts. He gently grabs them as he kisses me, he lifts me up with my legs still around him, carrying me into my bedroom. He throws me on the bed and pulls my legs around his waist. He kisses me from my chest to my torso, exploring my body. He then pulls down my shorts, looks up at me, pleased that I'm not wearing any underwear.

He places his face in between my legs, kissing my inner thighs, then pulls me into his mouth. I gasp at the sensation, my body twitching with excitement and pleasure. At the sound of my moan, he opens his eyes and looks up at me. *Oh my, he knows what he's doing,* I throw my head back. He comes up slowly, kissing me everywhere, his lips and tongue brushing my nipples.

Once he reaches my lips, he inserts himself into me, his thrust starting slow and soft then becoming harder and faster, while waves of ecstasy rush through me. I gasp out of sweet agony. After we both climax. He rolls over, breathing heavily. I marvel at him watching his glazed, bronzed, chiseled chest rise and fall. *My God, he's beautiful.* He looks at me and we both let out a chuckle, he tells me to come closer. I immediately bury my head in his chest, wrapping my arm around him.

Five minutes later, we have sex again. We eat some pizza, watch TV, then do it a third time, with me on top. After we are done, we cuddle for a while, and he falls fast asleep. I thought this would help me forget. But I lie awake, unable to stop thinking about what happened last night, Lucas, and how it all began.

25

Karma 8 years ago

WHILE MY MOM is in jail, I have to stay with my grandparents, which means changing schools. I'm excited about the change. This means I can have a fresh start and be a new version of myself. I get to school and after a couple of weeks I figure out who's popular, who the weird kids are and everything in between. I instantly become friends with this girl named Katherine. She's well-liked especially by the boys.

Katherine and I hit it off immediately. She invited me to her house last night and several weekends before that. At her house, we usually just FaceTime her friends, both guys and girls or visit online chat rooms. The boys rarely pay attention to me, when they do it's usually to ask about Katherine. It's kind of frustrating, but attention is attention. I have a class with Katherine's boyfriend, Blake, we have art class together. They just started dating yesterday, she mentioned it to me at lunch.

At the beginning of the school year, they assigned Blake and my seats next to each other because of our last names. When we got assigned, he scuffed and rolled his eyes. Then he asked the teacher to sit in the empty seat next to his friend. I was so embarrassed I wanted to crawl out of my skin. I pretended I didn't hear it and kept my head down.

Despite that awkward first impression. Blake's been so polite to me since then, always apologizing if he bumps me and thanking me when he borrows a pencil.

He's quite cute. He has big brown eyes, thick tight curly hair, pretty lips, a wide perfect smile, and a button nose. After I got to know him first. I never told Katherine I had a crush on him, because frankly she has a big mouth and I didn't want to be humiliated again.

But I'm the one who sits by him in class and initially, I felt slightly betrayed. However, after he started dating Katherine, he began talking to me more often. He asks me what I think about his drawings and he compliments me on mine. Occasionally, our elbows touch. He even talks to me outside of class now, mostly about Katherine, but the way he looks at me makes me blush. We also share my colored pencils, he playfully bumps me to mess up my coloring, laughing as he teases me. He's actually really nice and smart.

With Katherine's birthday coming up, Blake asks me what I am doing after class. I get excited. Art is our last class of the day. I tell him I have no plans, he asks if my parents would mind. I lie and say no. They would, but they never know what I'm doing anyway, or care to know.

Then he asks for my number, I give it to him.

He takes me to the mall with him and we go shopping in his big red truck. He's so thoughtful, he even opens the door for me. Blake asks me what I think Katherine would like for her birthday, I instantly say clothes and makeup. He nods in agreement then we go to the makeup store.

Blake asks, "How would we know if this would look good on her?" Then he mentions that Katherine and I kind of look alike. I never thought about that. What does that mean? That he thinks I'm cute, too? It must be if he thinks we look alike, I blush. He tells me to try on a few lipsticks and after the third he exclaims.

"Wow, that looks so good. We're getting that one!" My stomach flutters. We buy lipstick and matching lip liner then we head to the clothing stores.

As we are shopping, Blake looks down at his watch and said, "Oh no, I'm going to be late for practice. Let's just grab these dresses in your size and we'll figure the rest out later."

I say okay, pick out the few I thought were cute, he buys them then drives me home. I don't tell Katherine where I have been, and it gives me a slightly satisfying feeling I have a boy secret. I like this feeling. The next weekend is her birthday party. Blake texts me saying he's here so I tell Katherine to go look for something in her room to stall her for a moment. I text him to come in and the coast is clear.

Then I stare at the door and wait till Blake comes in with the shopping bags, he motions me to go upstairs with him to try on the dresses, to see if they fit. Once we get upstairs, I grab them then ask him where I should change. Hoping he says in front of him, I wonder if he would like my body.

Then he says, "Um, I'll just turn my back. We don't have a lot of time. I hope she likes everything. I never know what to get someone for their birthday. I got her a cake, too."

As I'm finished putting on the first dress, I tell him, "I'm ready."

He looks at me up and down, raises his eyebrows, nodding. "That's nice and sexy, I like it." He sits down on the bed.

I'm flattered. He thinks I'm sexy? As I walk toward him, he smiles at me. I need to act now or I'll regret it forever. I knew him first. I kiss him. He kisses me back for a second, then pushes me away standing up.

"Karma, what the—?" He wipes his mouth. "What are you doing? I was talking about the dress. The dress— I don't like you—like that, and you. You are Katherine's best friend? What—" I just stand there stiff with embarrassment. I cover my mouth, in shock, and I run out of the room. I thought he liked me? I hope he doesn't tell anyone. Oh my God. As I run down the stairs I bump into Katherine.

"Hey, where have you been—" She pauses and gasps as she looks at my face. "What's wrong?" She looks genuinely concerned. Which makes me feel even worse, because I just tried to hook up with her boyfriend. I try to come up with something quick. Because I have the advantage of talking to her first.

"He tried to hurt me. While I was helping him with your presents, he tried to kiss me. I pushed him away, because you know, you're my best friend and then he got so angry, he slapped me," I whisper to her. Hoping she believes me. I get a glimpse of myself in the mirror. I'm ashamed and disgusted at my reflection. I'm looking at Katherine, trying to gauge her thoughts. Does she believe me? She just looks confused and hurt, not sure at who just yet.

Then Blake comes down the stairs, and she yells at him to leave and that they're over. He tries to explain and points at me. She yells over him, calls him a liar and tells him he needs to leave. Katherine hugs me and asks me if I'm okay. I tell her I am fine, and I just need a drink. The rest of the night we drink cheap beer. And she keeps getting calls from Blake over and over.

She blocks him, and keeps saying how sorry she is, and that I'm such a great friend. I smile as I swallow all the guilt and embarrassment of the past 3 hours. After the weekend is over, I go into art class late because I'm nervous, and I don't want him to be mad at me. I get into class and he is there in his regular seat. When he sees me, he shoots me a disgusted look, shakes his head, and ignores me.

The next day, he gets his seat changed. I don't know

what he said to the teacher but it seems he's got his way. I tried to apologize to him, but he won't talk to me. I even tried to text him. I need to talk to him. I feel so bad. I want to make sure he's okay. That's when I get the idea of making a fake account. I really like him and I miss his laugh, sense of humor and everything.

So, I went home that night to log out of Facebook on my laptop and make a new account and email. I picked the name Anastasia because I feel like it sounds exotic. I go online searching for a pretty, skinny foreign girl, with blonde hair and light eyes. Because that's the American beauty standard, right? The complete opposite of me. I search through a couple photos until I find the right one that hasn't been shared a million times, and this account has many super believable photos. I made friends with a bunch of random people that also live in Sydney by just looking up Sydney, Australia, mostly men, because I know they would be eager to have someone that looks like that as a Facebook friend.

I wait a couple of days to build my account with an adequate amount of friends and posts. By the same time next week, I friended him and one of his friends so it won't seem so weird. I'd say I saw them play at a football game, and I thought he was cute. Because he has his football number and school in his bio. That's not very safe in today's age. I check the account every hour. Nothing. Maybe he's still heartbroken about Katherine. But there is no way he liked her that much if he was flirting with me like that. A few days later, I get a response. I tell him what I rehearsed. He is flattered and says I am cute, too. We talk every day after that.

A few weeks later, when I am at Katherine's house, she is telling me about this new guy she is talking to, Shane, and that he asked her to send him nudes.

Then I got the idea to send Blake some. I don't really have any boobs yet, probably another reason he doesn't like me. Her body looks a lot like the girls' photos I have been using. She has a lot of bikinis and mirror pictures I have used. Her page had only ten thousand followers and like fifty pictures. I need to do something because he hasn't been texting me as much, especially after he asked me to go to his game and I flaked twice. I told him I'd be there and then, at the last minute, made up an excuse.

Since then, he has been taking hours to respond and his responses are one-word responses; super dry. So, I feel like I'm losing him. Now I'm desperate. I ask Katherine to use her phone, because mine is dead and I need to tell my grandma what time to pick me up. She hands me her phone and my heart beats out of my chest. I need to distract her for at least a few minutes. I look around.

"Do you know where I put my shoes?" I asked. As she looks around, I go through her camera roll. I don't see any nudes. So, I just go to her texts, click his name, Shane, then I can see all the photos they have shared. I send them to my phone one by one. While she still looks for my shoes. I then delete the texts between me and her. Then I hear my phone go off ding, ding, ding as the photos go through. We both looked at each other as she furrowed her brows, confused.

"I thought your phone was dead?" she said

"Me too! Ha-ha oh wow it came back to life." I try to laugh off.

She gives me a weird look and snatches her phone. "You know that day, my birthday party, why did you change into that dress?" she says.

"I-I don't remember." I try to change the subject "How did you do on your math test? I failed ha."

"I did fine." She says shooting me a look. She doesn't bring it back up the whole night, thank God.

A few hours later, I go home and text Blake those pictures. He likes them and says I'm so sexy. I ask him to send some. He does, of his body after the shower. Then he sends a picture of himself, with only a towel around his waist; I can see a print of his penis, it's hard. I giggle in awe. Blake is so perfect.

Then he keeps asking me when I am going to come see him. I don't respond. I don't have an answer. This is going to be harder to keep up than I expected, I probably need to stop talking to him. But he makes me feel good. No boy texted me before I started talking to Blake. He's the only hot guy that will talk to me. It's the only thing lately that makes me happy.

A few days after that, Katherine's at my house getting ready for homecoming. I go to the bathroom, when I come back Katherine's on my laptop, she sees all the messages from Blake. She also notices that the name and picture on the Facebook profile isn't mine. She confronts me about it, and everything that happened at her birthday party. She calls me a freak and a liar. Then threatens to tell everyone at school.

I panic and yell at her. "I have your nudes! I will spread them all over school if you do!"

"No, you don't!" she shakes her head in disbelief.

"You want to try me? Don't you remember when you let me borrow your phone to text my grandma?" I say matter-of-factly.

Now I feel like she believes me. She storms out of my room and calls her mom. Then she sits outside on my front porch for about twenty minutes waiting for her mom to pick her up. I think about going out there, but what will I say? Later, I text her to say sorry. I regret what I did. Three hours later, she still hasn't responded. I decide to call her, but the line just rings over and over. I look up what that means, and it basically says I was blocked. Wow!

After that I stop going to school. There's no way I can face her. Then who would I hang out with, eat lunch with? All of my friends are hers and frankly I like her more.

I still wake up early in the morning and leave at seven a.m., like I'd usually do for school to catch the bus. But now I just walk around the park a block from my house, and just sneak back in after my grandpa leaves to go to work at nine a.m.

After a week the school sends in a letter talking about my outstanding absences. He finds it and opens it as we all eat dinner. I then cry to my grandpa and beg him to get me homeschooled, because I am getting bullied tremendously. I tell him girls laugh at me, calling me ugly, and a loser every day. He believes me and consoles me as I cry against his chest. He agrees to me being homeschooled. I will finish school in the next eight months.

I don't talk to Blake anymore because every time I see him, it just reminds me of everything that happened and how much he doesn't *actually* like me. I still can't believe he pushed me away like that. Am I that ugly? Now I get to reject him back as Anastasia. I tell myself I'm going to delete it now that I got some revenge. But I keep getting so many messages in my inbox and so many likes on my pictures. It's just nice to have notifications.

Now that I'm out of school, every once in a while, I run into an old classmate at the supermarket. They ask me what happened, and why I'm not in school anymore. I'm surprised she hasn't told everyone yet. She can't possibly believe I would spread her nudes.

I know what happened was crazy, but we were actually friends. We loved each other. I guess her thinking I'd actually do that is better than her telling everyone that I made a fake account to talk to her boyfriend, after he rejected me.

I tell them I switched to online school to graduate faster, to start college sooner because I'm really focused on my career, and already got so many offers from so many colleges. Which isn't entirely a lie. My academic performance is excellent. I have offers. I need to get out of this town asap. A new start is what I need.

26

Karma

THE POLICE FOUND HIM. They found Lucas. I found out today at work the cops were there, the beach house Athena rented. The news was full of it, and everyone was talking about it, because they found him on the beach behind the house where we were partying. Now they are questioning everyone on the second floor in the glass room. That seems like a brilliant spot for everyone to judge their reactions.

They haven't called me in yet. I wonder if Athena has said anything about me, my heart beating out of my chest. I thought the rocks would hold him down. How did this happen? My head is spinning. This is my worst nightmare. I run to the bathroom and then I see Mr. Kelp staring at me. I look at him and he moves his gaze. The moment I walk into the bathroom, I regret it. It's filled with girls talking about Lucas. Their eyes widen when they see me.

"Karma, can you believe it? Another person dead?"

"Murdered," another girl adds. I shake my head.

"No, this is so crazy, it makes me think there is some curse or something," I say, trying to deflect.

"No, not a curse. There is a serial killer!" another girl says.

While the first girl rolls her eyes saying, "There have to be three victims before it's a serial."

It makes me think how nonchalant Athena's being. What if she's done this before. The way she acts is far from normal. Well, maybe someone else could say the same about me. I was with Brent all night yesterday, that helped distract me from everything. But why is Athena so calm? Is it because of what happened to her sister and friend that just caused her to be numb to everything? I'm uncertain.

This bathroom is driving me crazy. I have to get out. I came in here to sit with my thoughts and escape for a minute, but there are too many people, so I just wash my hands and pretend that's why I came in here.

By the time I get out, the police have left and said they will call or return later, and for us to present a list of the names of all the people that attended the party that night.

After we get released, I try to find Athena. I haven't seen her all day. I look around and I can't find her, so I go outside and call her.

She answers immediately, "Hey, I'll talk to you when I get home okay, at my place." She hangs up.

That was rude. Oh, she probably did that because of

the cops. That's smart. But I wouldn't say anything incriminating on the phone, but whatever, I'll just head home on the subway. Ray gave me more homework to do. This project is for another rebrand; I'm supposed to do some research for him. I don't know how I'm going to get that done, with everything going on. I'm so stressed out and anxious, I keep looking over my shoulder. Thinking that I see Lucas everywhere.

His curly blonde hair that just goes half an inch past his ears, big green eyes and thin lips. Broad shoulders and stout athletic build. He was so handsome. *I walk past five men that look just like Lucas. I feel like I'm seeing things.* I have feelings that I can't quite figure out, I'm mourning him, but I also feel like I survived him.

With that, I feel somewhat betrayed by him. How did he not understand that it was me, and my love was genuine? He fell in love with me, the texts, the calls, the sex, that was me. That's what he fell in love with, not the random girl in that picture. It hurt me that he couldn't see that. And he nearly choked me to death after he said he loved me, and always would. It's just ugh, like I know what I did was wrong, but he wouldn't have talked to me as Karma. I knew we would get along, fall in love, like we had.

We get to my stop, which interrupts my thoughts. I walk to the apartment and knock on Athena's door with no answer. I knock again. Nothing. Could someone have arrested her? No, if anything, I just beat her here or they asked her to come in. She's too smart to end up in trouble. I go to my place. Brent's not here. Then I see his text. It says he's at work and will be back late. I lay down motionless, thinking about how me and Lucas first met.

27

Karma 4 years ago

I THOUGHT my life would be more interesting since I'm a freshman in college. To my disappointment it's not, especially my love life, so I downloaded a dating app. I got a few matches, no one was really cute, then I saw Lucas.

His bio was so funny and he's a Pisces. He lives two hours away from me! His pictures were so adorable. He has such a nice body, athletic build with curly blonde hair and a big smile. It looks like he played soccer and football in high school. He has a picture of him shirtless catching a football, and a picture of him all hot and sweaty in his soccer uniform holding a trophy. He is so hot, and he has good music taste as well. I super swipe on him.

After swiping on him, I check the app day after day, after day. I try to convince myself that he has deleted it or something. Then I make one of Anastasia, just out of curiosity and I swipe all day until I find him again. I use my only super swipe on Lucas, and we match instantly. Which hurts my ego a little. Why didn't he like *my* pictures? The bio was the same as Anastasia's. He still never picked me. I'm indifferent to my feelings. I closed the app and cry myself to sleep, unable to stop thinking about him.

He messages me. "Hey pretty girl, how are you?" It makes my stomach flutter, and then I have to remind myself he's not really talking about me, let alone to me. I block those thoughts out.

Then I look at his bio again. He's a statistics nerd just as much as I am. We like most of the same music, and we are both studying marketing. So, I replied to him. We go back and forth, then he asks me to talk on the phone. I gave him my number. Five minutes later, he calls me, I answer and say nothing. I'm too nervous.

Then he says, "Hello?" And I say hello back in an Australian accent. I don't know why.

He says hello again and I say, "Hi is Anastasia," in an Australian accent. Then he asks about it, I lie even more, and say I'm a foreign exchange student. He says my voice is sexy. I can't help but giggle. Why I started talking with that accent is beyond me. I'm guessing, my rewatching of the Australian mermaid show is why. I wish I could be a mermaid.

We talk every day. He laughs at my jokes. He picks up on my banter, then throws it right back at me. We talk on the phone every night for weeks. I tell him about my mom going to jail, my grandparents, and life as an only child. He tells me about his older sister, how they are best friends, and how his parents divorced because his dad was an abusive drunk.

Then on a random Wednesday, I notice he hasn't replied to me for two days. I feel my heart grow empty. I call and text, getting nothing. I am heartbroken

Saturday morning, he calls me crying, saying his best friend died in a car accident. Not knowing what to say. I paused for a while on the phone, and just listened to him cry. I then say I lost a friend too, my best friend Katherine, a year and a half ago.

"Oh," he says, sniffing. "I'm sorry, how did she pass?"

"Breast cancer, and we were all surprised because she was still in a training bra."

He laughs. He apologizes for not calling.

"It's okay, I did the same when my friend passed." Katherine's not dead, of course, but I lost a friend, a best friend. I know how that feels at least. She won't talk to me anymore. I'm sure she hates me now.

He then continues to beg me to FaceTime after I have already told him my cameras broke. Which is a lie, I just can't let him see the real me: the girl he swiped left on. He refused to give me a chance. Every time I think of it, it makes me hate him, and myself a little more. I try to repress those feelings, but it comes back in spurts.

Later he tells me he has been saving up for a phone for me, so we can FaceTime. And that it just got delivered to me at the post office, because he really wants to see my beautiful face.

The next day, I pick up the phone from the post office and I try to come up with a plan.

I text him,

> Thank you, I got the phone. I'm swamped all day until tonight. Then we can FaceTime.

> Hey babe I'm happy you got it. I have practice til 7 then Im free

> Okay baby I'll call you then! :)

> Perfect, I cant wait to see your face beautiful!

> Me neither! <3 I love you, thanks again!

> No problem babe. I love you too!

I go to the wig store to find a pretty blonde wig that looks just like Anastasia's. After a couple hours, I find one, then I get some lipstick that she wears in the pictures. When the night comes, I put Vaseline over the camera, and dim the light. When he answers he looks so perfect and sweet. It works. He suspects nothing.

After a few months, he wants more. He wants to meet in person. I keep making excuses that I have class, homework, birthdays and holidays. But one day he tells me he's going to be in my town for a game, staying in a hotel. Then I conjure up this lie that the fraternity at my college is having a masquerade party and that I will come over after.

We have sexted before, talked on the phone about all the dirty things we'd do to each other, and I've been wanting this so badly. So, when the night comes, I wait until midnight to call a taxi to his hotel. I change in the hotel bathroom, putting on my wig, my tiny red tight dress with spaghetti straps and spray some sweet floral perfume called *Lust*.

Then I put on my masquerade mask that covers half of my face. It's black leather with intricate embellishments, and the upturned ends give it a Catwoman-like allure, making me feel sexy. To make myself look more like the girl in the picture, I over-line my lips with red lip liner, put in green contacts, and contour my nose and cheeks.

I head toward the elevator and press the button for the third floor. I'm so nervous, I practice my accent as I go up. On my way to his room, I walked by a few people. They all stare at me with judgment. His room is all the way to the end. Room 335. I knock on the door, my head down.

Lucas greets me wearing a white tank top and basketball shorts. He looks so sexy. He hugs me excitedly. I hugged him back. As he hugs me, he says how happy he is to see me. I say the same, then he kisses me. He grabs my hand, leads me to the bed, and we sit on the end beside each other. His room is dark, which is perfect, with nothing on but the TV. We talk for a little, then he asks me to take off the mask.

"No, I think it's hot. I feel sexy, like Cat Woman. What do you think?" I say as I stand in front of him, raising my arms and swaying my hips like I'm dancing at a nightclub, so much that my mini dress rises. He smiles, biting his bottom lip and grabs my hips to pull me closer till my legs are between his. He then kisses my upper thighs and looks up at me.

"Can I?" He reaches up my dress on both sides of my hips, gripping my underwear. I nod.

He pulls them down until they're at my ankles and puts his mouth in between my legs, I groan. His touch sends tingles down my body. I have felt nothing like this before. I grab his hair while he rubs his tongue against me, between my legs. Then he looks up at me, and I can feel a rush through my body, so uncontrollable.

He then stands up, pushes me against the wall, and puts his fingers in between my legs, rubbing against me, then inside of me while kissing my neck.

"Oh, you are so wet," he says against my mouth, breathily.

Then grabs both of my legs, laying me on the bed, reaching over to the nightstand to grab a condom. Looking me in the eye as he rips the condom open with his teeth. He then puts himself inside of me. Letting out a deep moan as I open my legs wider, welcoming him into my body. He thrusts inside of me eagerly, until he finishes. It didn't last long, but it was the most fun I have had in college. I have never felt so wanted and loved all at the same time.

The shower going off wakes me up around five am. I'm still in bed, naked. I wake up in terror because I didn't recognize where I was.

Remembering what happened last night, I smile and kick my feet a little. I feel my face for my mask. *Oh no.* It's not on my face, and I can't really see anything in the dark. Did he see my face? Maybe not, the sun isn't fully up yet. I tap my head to see if my wig is still on, it is. Crawling to the floor, I search for my mask and clothes.

I need to leave before he's done showering. I scramble around and find my dress and my phone. As soon as I hear the shower stop, I run out. Without shoes. I run to the lobby bathroom; I stay inside until my taxi arrives. It's too risky for me to wait in the lobby, he could see me. I get a notification that the car is here. I run out and get inside, then a sense of relief flows over me. I smile the biggest I have in years.

28

Karma

I WAKE up to the TV in the living room. I get up and I'm still fully clothed. As soon as I got back, I must have fallen asleep. I get out of bed and walk toward the living room. Brent's back, I see him shirtless on the couch all wide-eyed at the TV. He sees me.

"Karma, you have to see this! This happened when you were at that party!" my heart sinks as I rush over there to see the TV.

The news reports that the police have found Lucas on the beach right below the house we were renting. They also mention receiving new information from Lucas's friend, who informed the police that Lucas planned on meeting his online girlfriend at this party.

Her name was Anastasia Roberts. My eyes widened in surprise; I never thought he would tell people about me. Which makes me feel kind of proud that he loved me. They say they discovered that wasn't her real name, and they are questioning the actual woman, Marta Collazo. She claims she didn't know anything about Lucas or any party, and that she has been victim to people using her pictures for years ever since she became popular online at the age of fifteen. She extends her condolences to the victims' friends and family. The police are actively investigating to uncover who is behind this account and the murder. Then the broadcast cuts to commercials.

"Wow, can you believe that? Why would someone use a fake account to invite him to a party? Just to kill him? Oh, maybe they wanted to come clean about lying, got rejected, then they killed him? That's insane. Maybe it was a man behind the account? Did you see anything weird that night?" He looks at me curiously, then he sees the look on my face. "Karma, are you okay? Your face is gray. I'm sorry, I know this is a lot to take in." He embraces me. "I can't believe some psycho murder was lurking around that party."

I weep. That's what he thinks of me, the real me. Once the police trace everything back to me, that's how he's going to talk about me to people, and on the news, with my mugshot, just like my mom. I don't know how all this happened. I finally have a boy that likes me, organically, and I still have to hide who I really am. He's going to be disgusted by me. Orange doesn't even look good on me.

My grandpa's gonna have a stroke after he finds out. I cry on his shoulder even more. He rubs my back and tells me everything is going to be okay. I calm down. I look up at him.

"It's okay, baby," he says. I look at him, wanting to believe him. I feel so safe in his arms. He is so handsome and tall that I have to stretch my neck to look up at him. He wipes the tears from my cheeks and kisses my lips. I kiss him back. We make out, our tongues rubbing against each other. So deep and passionate. We cuddle and change the channel and he tells me about his site supervisor. And how she drinks ten cups of coffee every day and smells like cigarettes every day. We laugh and talk about work for a while.

But then reality sets in, despite feeling guilty, I remind myself to live in the now and enjoy these experiences while they last.

I kiss Brent again. I can't ignore the fact that I still need to talk to Athena to work out a plan. I need to get that account deleted before it's too late. Is it already too late? I head to my room to search for my phone. Athena called three times. Then there is a loud knock at the door and then it pops open. *He didn't lock the door?* I rush over and she screams.

"Oh, what—Karma?" she laughs. I shut the door and push her out. Her laughter is still audible outside the door. Brent grabs his shirt and puts it on. I try to come up with an excuse, to tell her. She's already seen him shirtless, not much I can say.

I go outside to talk to Athena. I don't see her. As I'm walking toward her room, I find her standing in her doorway, door wide open. I jump. She looks at me unamused. I walk in and close the door behind me,

"They literally just found out about your fake account and your busy fucking?"

"I—" She looks at me with disbelief.

"Yes, the account you hacked, fucking delete it."

"I didn't hack it, as I told you!" she says.

"Then who? Come on, Athena you're a fucking liar, a pathological liar. What's up with all these random men, these secret calls, all those checkbooks with different names on them, and the weird fucking accounts?" I yell.

"I'm the liar? Didn't you use fake pictures to talk to a boy for three years? And yeah, I have men that do things for me, but they know exactly what is going on. I bet we can't say the same for Brent or the late Lucas, or should I enlighten him?"

I roll my eyes. "If you don't have the account, then who does?"

"I don't fucking know. I should ask you that!?" A loud knock disrupts us.

It's the police.

29

Athena

I WOKE up in the hospital, needles in my veins, tucked into a twin-sized bed with white sheets. An empty chair sat beside me. Groaning, I became aware of the pain radiating through my head, arms, and body. I had no memory of how I got there or what had happened to me.

Each day started with a pounding migraine. My stomach churned nonstop, forcing me to my knees around the toilet every time I tried to eat. That went on for three miserable days. The doctors barely gave me any pain medication, clearly suspicious of me. They kept asking what I usually "used,". They told me I overdosed and was suffering from acute hyperthermia. I couldn't even argue—I was too disoriented, too confused. They asked for my name, and I had no answer. When they pressed for my address, I told them I lived in a house, but I couldn't recall where it was.

After two weeks, they told me I had to leave. They

didn't bill me, declaring me homeless. The memory loss was apparently "temporary," though no one could say for sure. The doctor claimed I was competent enough to leave, advised me to stay hydrated, and sent me on my way. A physician assistant—a kind woman—handed me an envelope as I was discharged. She whispered for me to hide it and open it later. Dressed in the freshly washed clothes I'd been wearing when they found me—just a pair of leggings and an old band tee—I stepped into a waiting cab.

As the car pulled away, I opened the envelope. Inside was $500 in cash and a key to a motel room. My breath hitched, and tears welled up as I stared out the window. I tried to keep quiet, but silent sobs shook my chest.

How is this my life? How do I not know who I am?

A few days go by and I survive off of pizza and Chinese takeout. The motel called me earlier this morning, and said I have to check out tomorrow by noon. I don't even know where I'm going to go. I lost the sense of caring. But I think I figured out my name or at least the first letter. I have a K necklace on my chest. Maybe I'm Kylie, Kayla, or Kim. I'm not sure but I know my necklace means something. It's attached to my identity, my life. It's my most cherished possession.

30

Karma

THE POLICE ARE at the door. We open it, trying to act normal. Standing there is an older gentleman who looks like he's been doing this as long as I've been alive.

"Hello, are you Karma? The gentleman in your apartment said you might be here." he asks in a deep New York accent. He's clearly a local.

"Yes," I reply, my voice cracking.

"Would you mind coming down to the station to talk with us?" he says, more of a demand than a question. He then tells me I can either ride in the cop car or follow them.

I tell him I don't have a car, and he says, "Well, you're going to have to sit in the back."

Once we arrive, someone else is using the interrogation room, so I sit in the waiting room. My hands sweat, and I keep going over the story in my head, my foot shaking nervously. Fifteen minutes pass, and I hear the door open.

The cop says, "Thank you."

The woman replies, "My pleasure. Have a good night."

I stand up because I know I'm next. Then I see her, we make eye contact. It's Katherine Wilson. She knows. My God, she knows. I feel as though I've seen a ghost. *What is she doing in New York?* I stand there frozen. Then I see the cop. This one is young and attractive. Nice bone structure, high cheekbones, firm jaw, warm smile, and a dark brown buzz cut. He motions at me to come in. He's smiling at me, though I can tell he's fatigued. His eyes have that spark, it's clear he finds me attractive. It's so distinctive now, especially since I used to get the complete opposite reaction from men.

Typically, men wouldn't even notice me or they'd stare with an expressionless face, as if they were bored. This makes me a little more comfortable because at least he would be nicer to me. I am curious if he believes her.

"Would you like anything to drink?" he asks

"Yes, could I have a diet Pepsi?" I say with a smile.

He smiles back, nods as he gets up and leaves to go get my drink. This buys me at least a couple more minutes to collect myself. I take a few deep breaths, trying to calm my nerves. When he returns with my diet Pepsi, he introduces himself as Detective Kuang, then starts asking me questions, just basic ones like my age, where I'm from, when I got to New York and where I work. Then, he shifts to the murder investigation. He asks me what I did that night. I told him I was out partying, got sick, and spent most of the night in the bathroom.

"Do you usually drink that much to where you get sick?" he asks.

"No, I, um, ha-ha that's the issue. I never really drink so I don't know my limit, and I ate little beforehand so yeah um rookie mistake." I try to laugh it off. He does not laugh; he just shoots me a disapproving look. *Okay, I think the ounce of pretty privilege I gained has expired.* I straighten my posture.

"How do you know Lucas?"

"I don't," I say firmly.

"Do you know anyone that knows him? Because someone invited him to that party and all of your colleagues say they don't know him, so how did he get there?" he says.

I shrug. "I'm not sure. I was hoping maybe you guys figured that out already. Sorry I just- this is so sad. I haven't really processed what really happened. I still can't believe there was a murderer lurking around the beach house we rented."

"Who rented out the house?" he asks.

"Athena did, and invited everyone to commemorate the colleague we lost; Josh. Do you think there's a connection between these cases?" I ask.

"I'm not sure, but we haven't ruled out the possibility. Another thing, did you see anything unusual that went on that night?"

"I mean I was in the bathroom most of the night. I saw little to nothing, let alone remember." I am proud of my answer, wanting this to be over.

"Was there anyone in the bathroom with you, maybe making sure you were okay?" he asks. I hesitate. I'm not sure if me and Athena went over that minor detail. This could ruin our whole alibi potentially. Maybe I'm thinking too much into it.

"Um, yes sorry, Athena she did. She came into the bathroom and held my hair for me while I was, you know, then we left together," I say.

"Was she with you the entire time is what I'm asking," he says as his voice hardens, not breaking eye contact.

"I believe so, um, yeah, that night is foggy. I would say yes, hopefully you know. A good friend would, right?" I say and he nods.

"Sure. Um, last question, would you have any reason to believe that anyone would want to kill Lucas?" I get flashbacks of that night, his hand on my throat, the look of betrayal and rage in his eyes. Him yelling at me, rolling down the hill, all that blood. Athena screaming at me. I shake my head at him and shrug.

"Yeah, I wouldn't know. I didn't know him, never even heard of him."

"Okay, so what is this about?" he slides over a screen-shot of the Anastasia profile and the messages. I feel myself sweating again.

"I heard about that on the news. I don't know. He was talking to a woman online that was using a fake picture."

"Well, you remember your old friend Katherine Wilson from high school?" he asks, his tone casual. "Yeah, she said you are behind this account. Said you even used it back then to mess with her boyfriend when you guys were in high school. I'm sure you recognize her because I saw the look on your face when she walked out. You two even locked eyes. I could've cut that tension with a knife," he adds with a smirk, like he's caught me red-handed.

He was right, but had no proof.

"She bullied me in high school," I snapped, my voice shaky. "She made up those rumors because her boyfriend tried to kiss me, and when I rejected him, he hit me! You can ask anyone that was at that party years ago. I ran out, crying hysterically, with a huge red mark on my face." That part is true. After I bolted into the hallway, I hit myself in the face for being stupid so my cheek was red.

"She hacked into the account after the high school reunion, with a couple of friends. One of them works in tech now as an ethical white-hat hacker. When she saw the guy on the news, she called it in and came all the way down here from Texas to provide us with these," he says.

I start to cry to help sell my story.

"She was so cruel to me. She bullied me endlessly. Before that, we were good friends. She turned everyone against me, got everyone else to join in on the harassment. That is why I had to finish my junior and senior years online," I sob, struggling to breathe between my words.

I can tell he now either just feels guilty or just uncomfortable at me crying. Katherine did this. What a weird, twisted witch after all these years.

"Um, sorry I just have to ask."

I nod, wiping the tears off my face.

"Another thing, though." He waits for my reaction. I don't move or say anything.

"Your friend Athena is something else," he says, leaning back with a smirk. "I looked into her, her sister Serena, disappeared, presumed dead after five years. And Athena dated a big-time drug dealer, who she said allegedly abused her and basically kept her hostage. She testified against him with all these crocodile tears, then vanished with the money. The authorities couldn't do anything about it because she got immunity for testifying against him. She's a real wild card, huh?"

He pauses for a moment, eyes narrowing. "Did you know anything about this?" he asks.

"No, she has never told me, we have only known each other a few months, since I started working at Introspection. She doesn't share much about her past. I don't know."

"Well, maybe when she wasn't helping you in the bathroom, like you said. She could have been with Lucas? Right, is that plausible?"

"I don't want to say something like that. I don't know what happened," I say frantically. This is all a little too much for me.

"Okay, that's fine. Just think about what I said. If you think of anything else that might be valuable to the case just call me." He hands me his business card; I take it and leave.

As I walk to the subway station, I try to replay everything that happened. Does he believe Katherine and think that Athena and I did this together? By saying that, is he trying to get me to tell on Athena and indirectly expose myself? I think he's trying to manipulate me. Athena used to date a drug dealer? While I understand that, the rest of it seems far-fetched. I will have to look it up myself once I get home. Athena has sent me a few texts.

I don't have the energy to talk. I take the long way home to think. When I arrive home, I realize Brent isn't there, which fills me with a mixture of relief and disappointment. Then I see a note left that says, *'Got called into work. I'll be back later tonight. Takeout on me!'* He left twenty-five bucks on the counter. We planned on going to dinner tonight. I sigh, and I go straight to my laptop.

I look up Athena Drakos. Nothing pops up but her social media accounts, which are all private. I hesitate, wondering if it's strange that I want to add her as a friend on Facebook, especially after we just covered up a murder. Eh, I shrug it off. At this point, I've stopped worrying about how cool, calm, and collected she perceives me to be. I decide to send her a friend request.

Maybe I could dig up more about her if I figure out where she's from. On her Facebook page, it only says she lives in New York.

Next, I search for news about Josh's death. I found a

news article about it that includes his last name, Marks. With that I look up his Facebook account and scroll through his friends list. *He has to be friends with Dani.* Then I see it: she's listed in his bio as his partner. I click on her profile. Turns out they are from a small town called Village Hill, New Jersey. I go back to google and type in 'Village Hill New Jersey Athena Drakos'. That's when I found an article about her sister, Serena Drakos, who went missing.

This article includes a story about their mother, Evelyn Drakos, who apparently went to jail for abusing Athena. It mentions an incident where Evelyn slapped Athena in front of the police, calling her a liar.

Following that, Evelyn was admitted to an insane asylum for a week before serving three consecutive weeks in the county jail. Afterward, DHS intervened and placed Athena with her father, Zeus Drakos.

I looked up the mother, Evelyn Drakos on Facebook. I only see one post; it's a picture of the missing poster with Serena Drakos face on it. With a phone number on the bottom. It's nine p.m. right now. I don't think it's a good time to call. I'm not even sure if that number is still in service, it was five years ago, but I've had the same number since I was in middle school. I'll just call first thing in the morning.

After I shut my laptop, I hear someone knock at my door. I freeze, then it opens. It's Brent, he jumps at me, I yell and he laughs. I slap his arm and tell him not to do that without laughing. Then he kisses me and asks me what I want to order. I say Indian food. I haven't eaten all day, because stress makes me lose my appetite. We eat takeout while watching cartoons. When we finish our food, we shower together. I love being around him. He makes me forget about all my problems. We have sex again and again. He falls asleep. I lie awake.

31

Athena

Now I know I'm a smoker. There is this girl I see every night outside by the dumpster under the flickering streetlight, smoking. The motel I'm staying at faces the highway. From my window, I have a perfect view of her. She's usually just looking toward the traffic. She's so tall and pretty. Her outfits are so cool, they're more like costumes with her candy-colored stiletto heels, fishnets and black pleated miniskirts with a sparkly tank top that is cut low.

Her outfits are always some variation of that. She seems so ethereal and majestic. Her demeanor is like a black cat. I only ever see her out smoking a cigarette or on the phone with someone. Or doing both at the same time.

After seeing her again last night, I decided that I'm going to get some cigarettes and smoke with her. God knows I could use a friend. I see her appearing from my window, I quickly throw on some clothes, run to the corner store and grab some cigarettes. They ask for my ID. I pretend like I left it in my other pants, along with my wallet. I bat my eyes. The one other thing that comes naturally. I have nothing now but my looks. The clerk looks around and gives me a coy smile as he slides over the cigarettes across the counter. I thank him and skip out of the store. This is the first time I have felt joy in a month. I peek over to see if she is still there. She is! I walk toward her, opening my cigarette box.

"Hi," I say, approaching her.

She just side-eyes me over her shoulder. I didn't expect that.

"Sorry I just wanted to see if you had a lighter," I say.

Her eyes light up and she smiles. "Yes, I do!" She pulls out a lighter and helps me light my cigarette.

I am not sure if I have ever smoked before. I take a hit and to my surprise. I don't cough; my body knows me more than I do. Feeling incredibly relieved, I realized I've been craving this for a while without even knowing it. She asks me my name. I tell her, Kylie. She then points at my necklace and I nod, smiling. She tells me her name is Sasha. I compliment her outfit. She tells me she's a dancer, and we hit it off. She asked me to come to the club with her that night. I have nothing else to do.

So I go, then she brings me on stage with her at the club as a dancer. She let me borrow her clothes and we ended up getting really close. We even became roommates. It takes me a couple weeks, but I end up making a lot of money. Money that I don't really know what to do with. I like working here, the girls are cool. I have been working here for a few years; I haven't had any problems with anyone. Besides this one girl who just started a few weeks ago at the club that keeps staring at me...

32

Karma

I CALLED ATHENA'S MOTHER, Evelyn, from the phone number on the flyer at five am. I haven't slept and Brent's still in my bed sleeping. I feel like this is the earliest appropriate time I could call. Because I feel like four a.m. is like late at night territory, and five a.m. is the early bird vibe. McDonald's starts serving breakfast at this time, anyway. So, it's completely justified.

I pace the living room while the phone rings and rings. No answer. I call again, maybe I should leave a voicemail but what would I say? "Hi, I'm your daughter's friend um she's the prime suspect in a murder case. Um, call me back please, I have questions?" I think that's kind of crude, but true I need her to answer.

I have to know her perspective and how Athena and her sister were as kids. Maybe I should say I'm a journalist. Or that I'm a detective reopening the case? Wait, no, I think that is illegal. I need to sleep. I'm getting delirious.

I'm just going to call her and tell her the truth, well the partial truth. I call again, straight to voicemail. This time I leave one.

"Hi, this is Karma, a friend of Athena's. We are interns of the same company, Introspection. Could you call me back at this number? Thank you!" I hang up the phone, disappointed.

Then I get another idea. Dani. I contacted the jail holding her, they told me I could arrange a visit or schedule a call. I make an appointment for a visit later today. By the time I'm finished with that, it's six am and I go back to bed. Once I'm in the covers, I see how peaceful Brent is, he looks like a baby. I stare at him for a while, trying to savor this moment. Then I fall asleep.

Later at work, I get a call, followed by two more missed calls from a number I don't recognize. I glance at my phone, during a rare free moment. Everyone at work now has been so tense. Burying themselves in their work. Mr. Kelp made it very clear where he stands too.

"It's disrespectful, disgusting, and intolerable to gossip about the deceased. I shouldn't have to explain that to adults, but here I am!" He announced earlier, his voice sharp. "We are only here to work, and only work! So, I don't want to see anyone on their phones or wasting time gossiping in the break room!" He continued.

His words echo in my head as I sneak another glance

at my phone for a moment, making sure the coast is clear. I see the missed calls, but before I can investigate further, Ray calls for me. He has been keeping me busy all day with endless, mindless tasks. Fetching coffee, making copies, shredding paper, taking out his trash, faxing, and rolling up lunch orders. When am I going to actually do something again? Something exciting. I walk, dragging my feet. Half-expecting him to ask me to fetch him another refill. Once I get there, Ray springs up from his chair, grinning.

"Perfect timing! Here, take over for me for a few hours. I have a meeting with an important client," he says, grabbing his jacket.

I frown. "Can I not come with you? I think it would be a great opportunity for another person to vouch for the company!" I say enthusiastically.

Hoping he would say, yes, I don't want to sit here and answer his emails and think about the case that's going on. No, I need to be productive: to focus on my career.

"Um, no, I don't think you can. I would love to, but I need someone here to check my email and communicate with potential buyers, okay? Next time though, champ, next time!" He puts on his jacket in a rush, grabs his keys, and pats me on the head.

I sigh and slump my shoulders. Well, at least I don't have to run around getting orders. I have to stay here and be on email duty. Then that's when it hits me. I called Athena's mom early this morning. I completely forgot. That number, that's probably her number. I pull my phone out quickly and check. Then I hear Mr. Kelp come behind me.

"What are you doing on your phone?" he demands. *He is such a pompous fool.*

"Sorry, this is really important. I have to take this call," I say as I call the number back and head outside.

While I'm walking out, I'm looking around for Athena. I haven't seen her today. They are probably making her busy with work as well. I call and it goes straight to voicemail. Fuck, I try again and again. Then she finally picks up.

"Hello?" She sounds as if she just woke up, or smokes a hundred cigarettes a day.

"Hello? Hey, this is Karma, I called you earlier, and you called me back. I wanted to talk to you about your daughter. I'm a friend of hers, Athena," I say nervously. I didn't hear anything on the other side for quite a few seconds.

Then she says, "How did you get this number?"

"Yes, um, sorry from your Facebook, the post about your missing daughter. Sorry about that, by the way. Yeah, I just wanted to, um help you, um like just talk about everything, get more insight, and help Athena, um she's kind of not okay right now. I'm not sure if she told you or not. I figured I'd help by calling you." the other side goes silent then she says.

"I do not talk over the phone. Meet me at this coffee shop on the corner of Lincoln and Barlows on 5th street. At noon tomorrow," she says in her monotone voice.

"Okay, okay, thanks, I—" she cuts me off by hanging up the phone.

Oh, my God. What am I even expecting to find out? How did Athena end up like this? Was it because of her mother? Did her mother do something? She seems kind of crazy because of the news articles and things. Well, I bet people could say the same about my mom. Going to jail as a kleptomaniac.

Lost in thought, I turn around to head back to the building, Mr. Kelp is standing there, staring at me through the door. My heart skips a beat. Startled, I fumble to open the door, his cold gaze never shifting.

"Can I help you?" I ask awkwardly, forcing my voice to stay steady.

"You know something funny," his tone measured but ominous. "That account— the one that used a fake picture to talk to that dead boy—friended my wife on Facebook. A few weeks ago, around the same time we had that *meeting*. Don't you think that's *strange?*"

I feel my stomach turn and I sweat. But I try to not change my demeanor. "I don't know," I said, swallowing and shrugging. "That is weird. Is that all?"

"Are you familiar with him?" He steps closer, his presence menacing, trying to intimidate me.

I shake my head. Keeping my expression neutral.

"You want to know what I think?" he continues, lowering his voice. "I think you're behind that account. I think you are a pathetic backstabbing bitch that will do anything to get what she wants. I may not know if you killed that boy, but I have no doubt you played a role in it. With that," he adds, his lips curling into a cruel smile, "I'm kind of impressed. I thought you were all bark and no bite."

He lets out a dark chilling laugh, shaking his head. "Guess we're even now." He takes another step closer to me to where we are only 4 inches apart and he whispers,

"This is the last time we will speak; you hear me? Or you'll regret it, I promise you." His eyes lock with mine, burning with hatred.

I swallow my fear and try to conceal my emotions. I purse my lips together, not able to speak, and I nod my head fast.

Satisfied, he turns and walks back toward the building without another word. I stand there for a minute and gather myself.

33

Athena

ONE DAY that girl that has been staring at me just comes up to me and says all wide-eyed. "Sorry I was staring. You just look so much like this girl, and I wanted to find the flyer before I said anything to you. So, you wouldn't think I was crazy!" She points to this picture of someone who looks just like me. "Your name is Kylie I know, but many people don't go by their actual names here for many reasons but. Um, yeah, just wanted to make sure you're okay. I'm from Rutherford, which is where she was found by some dumpster, and I couldn't not say something," she says.

I stood there in shock.

In the middle of the club, I stare at the picture in my hands and tears run down my cheeks. *Someone was looking for me?* I run and get a cab home. Once I get home, I look at Sasha's computer. I look up *Rutherford, New Jersey missing girl*. So many articles come up, then I see a

Facebook post from the mother saying this is her daughter, and she's missing.

Along with the flyer, pictures showing the missing girl, who is named Serena. The missing girl looks just like me. *This girl is me,* I think. I don't remember what happened.

Then I look further, and there is another girl who looks just like me—almost. I'm a twin? I click on the link to each account. The one for Serena is inactive. The other account, the one for Athena, is active. She lives in New York City, working at a company called Introspection. I study her profile picture.

I continue looking through other photos on Athena's page. While I sit here staring at these pictures, I can attach memories to these photos. I remember my birthday party. That's what Kyle gave me... He gave me this necklace, my boyfriend's initial, K.

I cry more. I scroll through more pictures. I see photos of my aunt's wedding and then pictures with *me* and my sister.

I go back to one of the news articles that says Serena is the missing sister. Serena looks a lot like me, but I can tell that the pictures of Serena from the article are not me. I keep looking at the photos and their tags. Then I found a news article that shows "Serena and her sister, Athena, last summer." I study the photo along with the description in the article saying who's on the left in the photo and who's on the right.

The article also says the mother is unstable. I look at

more pictures on the mother's Facebook page, and I can tell the difference between me and the girl in her photos who is tagged as Serena, the missing sister.

Then I realized one thing for certain. The sister who is tagged as Serena, who is supposedly missing, is not me. The girl who is tagged as Athena in the photos is me. She has my smile and my necklace, the one I am wearing right now.

I don't know what to feel. What I do know, is that I will book the first flight out to New York City.

34

Karma

TODAY I'M MEETING with Athena's mom, Evelyn.

Athena has been nowhere to be seen since yesterday, and I have no idea what's going on with her. I thought about texting her, but maybe that's not in either of our best interests. What would I even say? I don't even think she likes me. After everything she said to me. She could easily throw me under the bus if she gets put into a corner. So maybe it's best to keep her at arm's length.

The last thing I want her to figure out is that I'm talking to her mother. Or what if her mom told her? Honestly, I doubt she even talks to her mother. I've never heard her mention her mom. It doesn't matter. I need to find out what happened to her sister.

Athena's behavior has been gnawing at me. The way she acted that night, like it didn't faze her at all. And the way she can switch her emotions on a dime... like when they announced our colleague's death, Josh. She was hysterical one second, then completely composed the next, even cheery. Calling a car to take us to her place, she casually started talking about all the fun things we'd do there, like nothing had happened. These thoughts swirl in my mind as I walk to the subway, trying to organize the questions I want to ask. I think I might just start very cut and dry.

When I arrive at the cafe, I'm looking around. The picture I saw of Athena's mother was over five years old. I wonder if she would look the same. She should look similar. I then look for just an older woman by herself. This place is really busy, and there are plenty of women alone on their laptops. Maybe she's not here yet.

I look at my watch and it is 12:06.

Then I feel a tap on my shoulder. I turned sharply, startled.

"Karma?"

I see a tall, thin woman. I can tell she's older, but she looks good for her age and youthful. She's pleasant, which differs from what I expected. Her long wavy strawberry blonde hair, held up with a clip and a few strands falling loose to frame her face, reveals a natural beauty. She's not wearing any makeup, but doesn't need it with her sun-kissed tan skin and rosy cheeks. She doesn't look crazy at all. I feel a little more at ease.

We sit down, and she starts with a polite, "How are you?"

I reply, "Fine. How are you?"

"I'm doing the best I can," She replies with a sorrowful smile.

A few moments pass in uneasy silence before her expression stiffens, her face growing serious.

"So, what do you know?" she asks abruptly.

I stumbled on my words not expecting her to say that.

"Um, uh, yeah, Athena told me her sister went missing a few years ago. When we ran into Dani, her old friend, she got really upset about it. And yea I just wanted to know more. Um, of course, if you don't mind because Athena's been a little off lately because of the stuff at work. So, I wanted to reach out to you, for some insight and support," I say, trying to sound believable.

She stares at me unimpressed. It's clear she doesn't seem to buy it.

"You know when I was first pregnant," she begins, leaning back in her chair, her voice calm but unsettling. "I had a strange dream. I dreamt that I had twins—two little girls. But one of them was evil. She killed the other by holding their head down, drowning them in the tub".

I blink unsure where this is going, but the chill running down my spine keeps me silent.

"In my dream, I put them in the tub and went to get them some toys for them to play in the bathtub together, you know like twin toddlers do. It took a while to find the toys I was looking for. Then I remembered I put them in the baby bag. I grab them, the two little duckies, and rush back because I know a mother is not supposed to leave two toddlers in the bath together alone, because accidents happen. But once I got back, I saw one of them had turned into a monster and there was blood all in the tub, and the other baby was face down, motionless."

Her voice is eerily calm as she continues.

"That dream terrified me. I was afraid I was carrying twins, and that one might harm the other in the womb, but when I saw the doctor, they confirmed I was only expecting one baby. I was so relieved." She pauses; her gaze distant. "Then months later, I was surprised to find I was pregnant again, even though I was on birth control. Now I understand why it happened. Don't you see?"

She looks at me now, her cold, dead stare locking me in place.

"The prophecy had to be fulfilled. They are the spitting image of each other, and one of them is a monster that got rid of the other. My dream. It came to pass. You see, she is the devil, she was born without a soul." She says with conviction.

"Um, what do you mean by that? What happened?" I ask my voice low and nervous.

Her lips curl slightly, almost like a smirk. "What do you think? You obviously know something's wrong with her by now, or you wouldn't be here, calling me from a Facebook post from five years ago," she says as she sips her water.

"I should ask you what she did to you." She chuckles. "But no, I'll amuse you, girl."

35

Athena

ONCE I GET to New York, I realize I haven't eaten all day. My stomach is in knots and I'm filled with rage. How could she do this to me? No one looked for me? Well, if so, not well enough, I wasn't that far. How dare she. I could easily cry for days. I'm heartbroken and in disbelief. Ever since I found out, I haven't slept. I have a plan now.

Not sure exactly how this is going to pan out, but it will work.

I first need to find out where she lives. I look just like her even after all these years. That much, at least, I can give her credit for—after all wasn't that her goal? I head to her apartment complex acting confused, tipsy and ditsy to the front desk clerk. It didn't take too much effort to connect the dots. I found out where she lived from one of her posts about this cafe that's right in front of her building. Luckily, it's a small distinctive mom-and-pop-shop and the only one in the area.

To my surprise I manage to get a spare key. My heart races as I step into one of the nicest apartments I have ever been in. She probably said the same, given that we grew up poor. The contrast is jarring.

I don't know what I'm looking for. But I know I'm looking for something of substance. I am still in a state of disbelief. Feeling manic. I throw everything around, screaming and crying. I'm trying to convince myself that she wouldn't do this, this can't be real and that I must be mistaken. But it is real, the room under my name that's already confirmed there, the social media accounts and everything. I lost it. Until I found what I didn't know I was looking for.

Her diary.

36

Karma

ATHENA'S MOM, Evelyn, tells me how she believes Athena made Serena disappear, by drowning her somewhere like in the dream she had—or maybe the other way around. She says she can't even be sure who's who.

"They looked identical by the time they got to high school," she says, her voice heavy with bitterness. "They even started wearing each other's clothes. They would fight over it—screaming at each other over tank tops, for goodness' sake. I even heard them threaten to kill each other over it once."

I nod politely, but I can't help thinking that siblings say things like that all the time. It's cliche in sitcoms, nothing sinister.

"You want to know how I know it was her that did it?" Evelyn leans in, her bloodshot eyes narrowing.

I shrug, unsure of how to respond.

"Because Athena didn't even tell me the first time

Serena didn't come home. I had to find out from the police. The POLICE came to my door and asked why Serena wasn't in school," She slams her bottle on the table, her voice rising. "I marched up those stairs to cuss her out, and to my surprise she wasn't there. I called her childhood best friend. She says she hasn't talked to her in months. I didn't know who else to call, Serena's always been a hermit, or *was a hermit.*"

Her words are slurred now, and I'm sure whatever's in her bottle isn't just water. The sour smell of alcohol lingers between us, and her dilated pupils suggest she's on something else too.

"The police stuck around all day, waiting for them to get home. I had to play *host.* I asked those pigs if they wanted tea or coffee. Thank God they said no. It was an empty gesture anyways. We just waited as we watched TV for what felt like an eternity. They even had the nerve to interrogate me in my own house, like I was some kind of bad mother or something." she takes another gulp of her drink, with no reaction but a burp.

"Finally, when Athena got home, I jumped up and said, *'Where is your sister?'* She walks in, gives this stupid shrug and says *'I don't know. Why, what's going on? Why are the cops here?'* I quickly walked toward her, grabbed her shoulders, looked her dead in her eyes and screamed, *'WHO ARE YOU?!? WHAT DID YOU DO TO YOUR SISTER?'* Then the cops stood up.

'Do you have any idea where your sister could be?' The cop asked, Athena said *'No.'* At the same time I said *'Yes.'*

I looked at her like she's lost her mind. She continues to lie, saying she doesn't know. We started yelling at each other, back and forth, and that's when everything clicked —from my dream. I lunged at her. They arrested me. And then she went to live with her rotten father. Even last week, she tried to sneak into the house and steal their birth certificates. Sly little girl. Can you believe that? I saw her on my security camera approach the house and walk toward their old bedroom. I walked over there and watched her rummage through those papers. I threw a plate at her, clicked my gun, and told her to get out of my house," she says.

"She jumped so fast, the plate even cut her neck— that felt so good. I got to protect my baby girl, in a way from that evil girl," she says with a twisted satisfaction, staring at me like she expects me to respond.

I meet her gaze, unsure of what to say. My throat feels dry, and my head is scrambled. *So that's where Athena has been.* I could use some of whatever she has in that bottle.

"Um, I'm sorry about everything. I have to go." I rise from the table, eager to leave. "Um, thank you again for meeting me. I'll... I'll be in touch." I say.

Before I can step away, she grabs my hand, her grip iron-tight. "Don't let her ruin your life too, or has she already. Is that why you asked to meet me? What did she do?"

I shake my head. "It's nothing. But I really have to go. Thanks again," I say, yanking my arm back.

I practically sprint toward the subway. Fuck. I still

don't know what really happened to her sister. But I don't know if I can even trust her mother. She seems off. Crazy even. She can't even tell her daughters apart. I want to get more information out of Athena. I need to see what she's up to and if the police have contacted her again.

I text her,

> Hey, can I come over in a little bit?

> If you're not busy.

> Sure

She texts back almost immediately. Once I get to our apartments, I go straight to her door and knock.

As I wait at her door, I realized I hadn't eaten all day. Today has been so crazy I forgot to eat. I hear my stomach give me confirmation. She opens the door greeting me cheerfully, like everything's okay. I look at her a little frightened and confused. What really happened to her sister, *did she do something to her*? How is she acting so flippantly about killing Lucas, and why does she hate her sister's best friend?

"What's up?" Athena's voice cut through my spiraling thoughts.

"Oh nothing, I haven't seen you at work lately. I just wanted to check on you, how are you doing." I say.

She looks up at me with a tight, forced smile. "Oh yeah, I had to go run a few errands that took longer than expected. But yeah, I'm fine."

"Okay, so have the police talked to you again?"

Her expression darkened slightly. "No—"

We hear a loud knock on the door. My chest tightens. It's the police again.

Oh no, have they spoken to her mother or even worse caught me talking to her mother?

"Hello, open up we need to talk to you," says the same detective, the older local one, not the attractive one sadly.

"It's Detective Larson." I open the door. Detective Larson and his partner, who I don't recognize, just stand there staring blankly.

"Me?" I say, as I can hear my heartbeat pulsing rapidly.

"No," the detective said firmly. "Athena."

"For what?" Athena snaps annoyed, as if she is getting called into the principal's office, and not to the police station.

"We have more questions for you that are pertinent," says Detective Larson.

Athena rolls her eyes, and says, "Okay let me grab my purse and stuff first." She takes her sweet time picking up her belongings, clearly testing Detective Larson's patience as his expressions tightens with annoyance. Then they walk out. And I realized I'm here alone.

I'm in Athena's place alone. I press my ear to the door, straining to hear if their footsteps had faded. Adrenaline is coursing through my body. I have to hurry.

What if she comes back up? If she finds me snooping, will she throw me under the bus? Or has she already? I do not know what she did with all the things she claimed she'd gotten rid of. I run to her bedroom and go into her drawers. I find nothing but notebooks and pens. The other drawers are just full of clothes and under the bed are boxes of shoes. I rummage through her closet, pulling at hangers and pushing past rows of neatly hung outfits. I found nothing from *that night*. Guessing that's a good sign, or maybe she hid it somewhere else.

Unsure what to look for, I circle back to the drawers and flip through the notebooks with nothing but phone numbers, names, and addresses. Receipts of mail also addressed to many people; it looks like credit card mail.

Then I look into another notebook. These are social security numbers with addresses and brief notes like "mother's maiden name". Is Athena a fraud? Is that what the police are asking her about? Well, at least I have something else on Athena if she tries to tell on me. I take a few pictures, for proof.

Peering into the closet, I spot a bin at the top, overflowing with more items. I look through it and I open more notebooks but these ones look different. They are old and cute with flowery covers in pastel shades of pink and purple, are these diaries? I open the first page.

"I realize I'm different from people my age."

37

Karma

I FINISHED READING the entire diary in one sitting. I'm shocked. I know so much and yet nothing at all. What is going on? How was she able to throw her sister away like that literally?

I'm dealing with a psychopath. I feel numb. In the middle of her closet, I just lie here. Time has slipped away from me. I have to get up and go. Grabbing the diaries and the tub, I pause and think I should take pictures of them. I'm taking pictures of the ones about Dani's mom and Athena. Shutting it, I try to leave things as I found them before running out. As I walk back to my room, I get a text from Brent.

Can we talk?

My heart drops. Does he know something? Did Mr. Kelp talk to him?

I respond quickly,

> Yes.. I'm home now.

> Okay, I'll be there in 5.

Is he going to break up with me? What if he was on my computer before everything happened and saw me logged in? I pace back and forth in my room. I want to crawl into the fetal position and just cry. Everything is falling apart. What am I going to do? I need to talk to Dani. They put her in jail for a murder that I think Athena committed.

Well, not "Athena," *Serena*. A murder that *Serena* committed. Who do I tell? I can't tell anyone. I can just tell Dani I know she was right, and what she did to her mom. Even if *Serena* would tell on me. No one would believe her, it would be me, her mom, and Dani against her and her diaries. I need to talk to Dani now, before it's too late. Athena, I mean *Serena* could be telling on me right now.

Then Brent walks in. "Hey," he says in a sorrowful tone.

"Hey," I say, trying to sound unbothered with a light smile.

"What's wrong?" he says. I'm guessing I look as bad as I feel.

I stand there unable to speak and I feel the water fill my eyes and I sob uncontrollably. This is too much for me to handle. The only cute boy that actually liked me is breaking up with me. I got my first love murdered, and he died hating me. I might go to jail and I know all these dark secrets that I can't tell anyone. All these dead, innocent people. And I can't do anything to help it. Brent's holding me as I cry into his chest. He pats my head and tells me it's okay.

"What do you mean it's okay?" I yell as I sniffle. "You're breaking up with me?"

Brent shakes his head with a sympathetic look on his face.

"No, no, I just feel you have been off. You ignore me at work, you're never home, and you barely even text me back." I look at him, confused. I don't remember him trying to talk to me at work or his texts.

"When?" I say, pulling out my phone. I do have a missed text. He texted me exactly when I sat down to talk to Evelyn.

"Oh, okay." I wipe my face and I let out a chuckle.

"And I tried to say hi to you when you were speed walking out of the building," he says.

"Oh, sorry, I had an important call, it was my mom, everything's okay with her though. She texted me, 'I need your help' and I was worried. I thought something was wrong with her, but she just needed help setting up her email. She forgot her log in and expected me to know it." I lied. Although that has happened before. Just not while I was talking to Athena's mom.

"Sorry," I continue, "this has all just been a little hard on me. The police are everywhere, and the murders are freaking me out. This has been a lot for me. It has absolutely nothing to do with you. You're the only good thing right now, and I don't want to mess it up," I say.

He pulls me in, saying everything is okay and that he is about to move out because he shouldn't have moved in, in the first place. "I still want to see you and spend the night here and there, but it's not right for me to live here. I want a clean slate, okay?"

I agree. He shows me pictures of the loft he is going to be moving into. He is going to be an old lady's roommate. Best deal he could find. He then tells me about how hard it is to find a place here and all the funny things that happened to him along the way. We laugh, and he cuddles with me.

I think I'm in love. I never want this to end. But for that to happen he can never find out what I did, who I am. As Mr. Kelp said, a 'pathetic back stabbing bitch'. I don't think that's entirely true of all those bad things I did. I was backed into a corner, which is why I did those things. The fake Anastasia account, I did that because I was lonely. But I tried to stop Lucas, he just wouldn't let me. I smile at Brent as he brings me a glass of water and a plate from the takeout we ordered. Takeout and reality TV is the best post-work combo. Tomorrow, I have a lot to do. I just received an email confirming my meeting with Dani. He sleeps over.

When I wake up, he's gone.

38

Karma

I PREPARE for my meeting with Dani, and get dressed. I'm curious to hear what she'll say about the diary. I call a cab. The subway is going to take too long. I barely make it in time. I walk into the jail. It's better looking than I imagined. It's a tall brick building with wide steps and glass revolving doors. I'm greeted by the front desk lady. She asks me my name and tells me to follow this officer through the door. Where I then have to walk, take off my shoes and put my things in a container. Then go through a metal detector. I walk through, grab my belongings, then I follow another officer to the meeting rooms.

This looks just like the ones in the movies. They point me to a seat to sit in and reiterate the rules. No arguing, no trying to touch the inmate etc. I don't think I could even touch her through this glass in between us. I wait a few minutes until they let her out. As I watch, she walks to the chair. I straighten my posture and pick up the phone. Her expression suggests she isn't happy to see me. I'm not sure if she even recognizes me.

Dani has her hair in a loose bun with pieces of her blonde hair out at the nape of her neck and near her temples, as if she had just woken up. She looks so different from the first time I saw her. Plopping down in her orange jumpsuit, that is two sizes too big, and puts the phone to her face. I wave with an awkward smile. Dani's face doesn't budge, lifeless.

"Hey, um I don't know if you remember me or not." I cleared my throat. How can I tell her that her childhood friend murdered her mother?

"Okay? And?" she says.

I can tell she's miserable. Who wouldn't be? She's in jail for a crime I'm sure she didn't commit. I mean I have no proof, but *Serena* has a history of killing people. I feel like she killed Dani's boyfriend because she felt like Dani was going to find out who she really was. Her comment about one of them being pigeon-toed has come back to me.

"Okay, I don't know how to tell you this," I whisper as I scoot closer toward her. "But I found something. I believe you. I don't think you killed Josh." Her eyes light up as she leans closer. "I found Serena's diary. She talks about hurting your mom and her sister Athena, who she is *pretending* to be." I whisper.

Waiting for her response I see her eyes grow big and her face frowns. She has this look of disbelief and hurt. I see her eyes fill up with tears.

"I always thought what happened to my mom was weird, but she had been sick for so long" she gulps trying to conceal her emotions. "We all expected it, but now that you say something, that bitch was asking all these weird questions about her medication and stuff before it all happened," she says as she wipes her face.

"I'm sorry, um, but which one of them did you say was pigeon-toed?"

"Serena is. You know once they both got to high school they looked like twins. I was gone for like a year. I had to move in with my grandma temporarily. Then my aunt took custody of me so I could be closer to my hometown and see my friends. Serena was always so weird though; she was so socially awkward. Until she grew out of it, I guess. Or just copied her sister. Once I got back, it was like they were carbon copies of each other. It's almost like Serena didn't know how to act unless it was just like her sister. She would wear her clothes, makeup and everything. It was weird, but after a while I got used to it and so did everyone else, I guess I just hoped Athena would come back. I didn't want to believe she killed her. I've known them my whole life." she shrugs.

The guard yells at us, "Three more minutes!"

"What does it say in there?" Dani asks.

"Your mom or...?"

"Both. Quick."

"She killed your mom by giving her too many pills, same with Athena."

I didn't even know how I was to describe that. I guess that works.

"You should tell your lawyer!" I say trying to sound somewhat remotely positive.

"Did she say anything about what happened to Josh?"

"No, she stopped writing six years ago. But I'm sure she did it, and you can help by testifying or something we can get her. I swear—" I say, cut off mid-sentence,

"The meeting's over in two minutes," the guard says.

"I'm sorry to tell you like this, but I had to tell someone, this is driving me crazy," I whisper into the phone.

"Tell me about it," she says in a lifeless whisper. "Make sure you come see me again. I just need some time to think." She puts her hand on her head.

I nod. She stands up, and the guard follows her back into the jail and she's gone. What am I to do now? My phone rings. I look down at the caller ID. It's *Athena*.

39

Karma

I CANCEL her call as soon as it pops up. She doesn't know where I am. If it's important, she will text me at least. She calls again; I ignore the ringing. I haven't decided where I am going, or what I will do yet. I'm sure she will ask. Everyone's on edge right now. I walk to the subway. I'll just go to her room and say I never got her call, and I went walking around to go sightseeing. Yeah, that's believable, there's always something to see in New York.

My heart is still beating so fast after talking to Dani. She seemed so out of it. So detached and disoriented. I can't imagine what she's going through. There's no way that can be me. I think I have more than enough evidence against Serena and it's my word against hers, well me, Dani's and her diary. I don't know how concrete that is though with Dani being a "felon" and the diary not being so credible. Anyone could have written it, but it's so detailed. If I could get her to confess, that would be the evidence, but how do I do that? Without telling her I read her diary, what if she tries to hurt me? Like she did with everyone else?

I have to remember I'm dealing with a *murderer* here. Someone that will stop at nothing to get their way. I get back to my room, collapse onto the bed, exhausted but unable to rest. Brent's gone. I miss him, his warmth, his touch—his body. I close my eyes and let myself think about him, the way his hands feel on me. For a moment I smile, lost in the memory.

Then my phone buzzes, jolting me back to reality. Just a notification about an email. I have to go see Athena. Hopefully, she's in her room. Summoning what courage I have left; I walk to her door. But I hesitate to knock on the door. My forehead rests against the door as I try to figure out what to say.

Before I can decide, the door creaks open beneath my weight. It wasn't fully closed. Worried and scared, I tiptoe as I hear a commotion in the bedroom. I freeze and the screaming gets louder. It seems as if she is fighting someone. I walk further toward her bedroom. It sounds like two women. My breath catches as I reach the hallway outside her bedroom. Suddenly, the door bursts open, and they tumble out, screaming.

My body freezes as something clatters to the floor near my feet. A gun. I scream as they stop and look at me. My eyes widened in shock, my stomach dropping. They look identical. It's them. I thought she was dead. I feel like I've seen a ghost.

One of them yells, "Karma! Help! Grab the gun! GRAB THE GUN!"

I'm paralyzed.

The other screams, "Karma, help me! Karma, it's me! She's trying to kill me! She drugged me! Karma, she's a murderer-shoot her!"

"Shut up, Karma! No! It's me! It's me!" she yells.

I can't tell them apart. I hold up the gun, pointing toward them. Shaking.

"She's trying to kill me. Karma. She drugged me. Karma. She's a murderer. Karma, shoot her!"

"Shut up, Karma! No, it's me it me. Karma, she broke in here. She's a liar! You know me, Karma, you know!"

They fight again.

I panic.

I shoot.

Two hours later

I don't know who I shot. I'm not completely sure what my motive was with the shooting. Besides stopping them. Two Athena's are too many.

The cops arrive quickly, separating us in the hallway of our apartment building. I'm struggling to breathe, let alone converse. Athena on the other hand is very calm and composed. She tells them what happened, her voice very smooth and unwavering. I'm not sure who she *is*. She seems so familiar, yet so much like a stranger at the same time. But that's not new. That's something about Athena's charm: she can make you feel like the most important person in the world, like you have known each other your whole lives. Then in a blink of an eye, she'll turn on you. Making you question everything you thought you knew about her. She's very manipulative that way.

The police again, escorted us to the police station. I have managed to calm down by the time we arrive. No longer shaking. Though my nerves are still raw. They ask me to recount what happened again.

"Athena called me. Twice and I didn't answer. Which I regret so much. I can't believe I didn't answer." I shake my head, sniffling.

"Why didn't you? What were you doing?" Detective Kuang asks.

I hesitate to answer. They don't know about the talk I had with Dani and the diary. Fuck the diary. That's the motive. They don't know I read it though. I have to talk to Dani after this.

"I was out in the city walking and sightseeing. I needed to get out of the house. With everything going on, I just needed to clear my head. I didn't want to talk about work or anything. I just wanted some peace. I just wanted some time to myself. I got a coffee in the city and got back on the subway. That's when I went into her room to talk to her to see what she called about, you know?" I say as my voice cracks.

Detective Kuang watches me closely, his pen poised over his notepad.

"Then what happened?

"I just heard screams and thumps and I was so scared I didn't know if she was getting robbed or assaulted by a man or something. Because the door was half shut, I didn't know what to think. Then I heard two female screams, and I tiptoed further, then I saw them fighting to the death and a gun slide from under them. I'm guessing that's what they were fighting over, and it slid to my feet. I froze, and then they started just yelling at me to pick up the gun and save her. So, I did. Then they kept yelling at me, then one of them got upset and fought with the other again, trying to kill Athena, so I shot her."

"Who? Who did you shoot?"

I don't know. But I can't say that. I have a good guess though, but I'm not one hundred percent sure.

"I shot the one who broke in with the gun, trying to kill my friend. Her estranged sister. She came back and saw that Athena had a good life, and she tried to kill her."

"How do you know? How can you tell them apart?"

I frown and meet his gaze. "Because she's my best friend, I would recognize her anywhere. I see her every day. I mean, I guess that would be difficult for you to tell them apart but not for me. We are very close, Athena and I," I say firmly, though the words feel hollow as I speak them.

He nods slightly and presses on. "Okay, well, something else I wanted to tell you. They found drugs in the person's system who was fatally shot. Do you know anything about that?"

"No, I wouldn't. I told you I don't know that woman. She could be on anything under the sun," I say. That could be true for both of them. But I can't let him see my doubt.

"Okay. I think you have answered all my questions. You can't go back to your place or leave town. We are going to need to have some follow-up questions after we search the crime scene."

"So, I can't go to my apartment?"

"No, we have to block off that entire hallway so there is no room for tampering with evidence.... you understand? Do you have a friend you can stay with in town?"

I hesitate. Then I think of Brent. He owes me one.

"Yes, I actually do."

The police drop me off at Brent's place. Once I step inside Brent's place he keeps asking me questions. I tell him I don't really want to talk about it. My story isn't straight yet. I can't let him know anything about what really happened. I tell him I'm just really tired and hungry and that I'll tell him everything in the morning. We order pizza. I eat and then fall asleep immediately.

40

Karma two weeks later

I DON'T KNOW if Serena is here or dead. They have cleared the crime scene, so we can go back home now. I didn't tell Brent that I can return to my apartment, he found out through Ryan.

When he mentioned it, I just acted surprised. The truth is I don't want to go back there. I have been trying to block it all out, pretending like it never happened. Brent has been pestering me to tell him what happened. I just told him what I told the cops. I rehearsed that story a hundred times in my head. It's mostly the truth.

But the fact that I don't 100% know who was taken away in that gurney makes me sick to my stomach. I hope it was *Serena*. The "Athena" I knew. I can't believe she managed to do all of that and get away with it for so long.

But even now, it's terrifying to think she can still fool me.

I act like everything is fine when I'm around her. I

keep trying to study her and see if anything is off. I wish Dani were here—she'd know. I need to talk to her, but I know I'm being watched by the cops and Athena. I can't even risk using my phone without worrying about it being tracked. Random people keep staring at me. I don't know if it's real or if I'm just being paranoid.

But I did kill someone in defense of my friend. I believe that counts as justifiable homicide in the court of law, right? I don't want to find out. I have been trying to gather more information, by asking Athena things that happened when we hung out last to see if it's *her* or not. But she always just dismisses my questions with nonchalant answers like "I forgot" or "I'm not sure" and changes the subject. Which seems like her, but then I think they grew up together. They know each other's personalities and according to Dani, Serena mimicked Athena through high school. So, Athena, being herself is inadvertently acting like Serena.

This is making my head hurt. I go to my boss and tell him I'm sick. I say I threw up in the bathroom and that my period is starting. He just shakes his head at me with a disgusted look and tells me to take the rest of the day.

Typical man—he doesn't want to hear anymore, basically gives me what I wanted just so I could stop talking about my *woman problems*. Men are so easy that way. I pack my stuff in a hurry, but not too much of a hurry so that I don't look sick. I hug my stomach and walk slowly with my head down for dramatic effect.

I rush to the apartment complex; I need to get into

her room. I have to find something, anything. This is driving me crazy. When I get to her door, I wiggle the handle. It's locked. Thinking quickly, I head downstairs to the front desk. I tell the receptionist that Athena asked me to go grab her purse. She left it in her room on the way to work. I show her my work badge and room key as proof.

The receptionist looks at me skeptically but seems to relax when she verifies my badge and key. She finally says okay and that I have to return it as soon as I'm done. I tell her I will, trying to sound calm as she goes and fetches it from the back. She's young, probably in her early twenties. She seems very naïve and overly trusting, which oddly gives me solace. Her attitude suggests she's had mostly positive experiences with people and their honesty, and for a brief moment, I admire that, maybe even envy it. When she comes back with the key, I thank her, with a big smile. As soon as I have it in hand, I rush to the elevator, adrenaline pumping.

Once I'm in Athena's room, I start at the closet. I don't see the diary. Why would she move her own diary? Is it here? Or did she move it for the investigation? Probably. I look everywhere under the bed in the drawers. This place is squeaky clean. I guess I would have moved it too if my room was getting investigated as a crime scene. Or that means I just have to look where no one would think to.

They escorted us out of here so quickly that we didn't have time to clean up. I think she did because this is what *she* planned. The real Athena planned to come here and kill her sister that was pretending to be her. So, she hid everything beforehand, then I showed up and killed *her* myself. I look in the fridge, the couches, then the plants. Nothing. Then I hear a rumble from the vent. The heat has turned on. It smells like something is burning. I walk closer and see that someone has tampered with it and scratched the paint. I drag the couch over to the vent in front of the door to step on and grab a knife to unscrew the nails and there it is.

The diary. The diaries......

I take them and put them in my purse. I'm not letting these go any longer. Then I try to get on her laptop but it has a password. Why is everything locked up so much? I have no luck with anything else. I leave. As soon as I make my way back downstairs, I get a call. The number is local, but I don't know who it is. I ignore it, return the key, and thank the lady again. Then the same number calls me again. Maybe it's Brent from a friend's phone. I answer it and it's Detective Larson. He says he has some news for me and that I need to come in for an additional line of questioning,

My heart rate is beating out of my chest. Am I actually being followed? Did they just see me break into Athena's room? Am I a suspect?

I get to the police office and I'm greeted by the same oddly attractive detective from the first time. He looks more disheveled than last time. This case is stressing him, I can tell. Maybe this is his first big case. He seems very young. Maybe twenty-five.

We greet each other with all that. *Hi, how are you* small talk bullshit. How does he think I am? I can tell he is not doing any better. He seems like the type of guy that puts his all into his work. He makes work his life. It seems like his life is very tumultuous at the moment, as is mine.

"I'm just going to get straight to the point, so the person you shot a few weeks ago. The doctors saved her. She is still unconscious though, but they say they expect her to wake up soon. So, if there is anything you have to tell me. I advise you to tell me now before she does. So, if you want to get your story straight, do it now."

"Her diary!" I blurt.

Detective Kuang looks at me, confused. I feel a weight lifted off my chest. It feels so good to tell someone about these demented diaries of a psychopath.

"Whose diary?" He asks, leaning forward with a skeptical frown as he taps his pen against the table.

"*Serena's,*" I whisper like it's a dirty secret. My hands tremble slightly as I clutch the diaries.

"Serena's diary? How did you get it?" His voice drops with disbelief.

"I stole it." I confess. "She has been creeping me out, so I looked through her stuff and I found all *this.*"

I put the diaries on the table and push them toward him. Relief washes over me as I watch him reach for the diaries.

He hesitates for a moment before he opens them

"How do I know these are real?" He asks.

"Ask Dani." I reply more confidently.

He looks at me and raises his eyebrows incredulously.

"The woman who murdered her boyfriend? She is your *viable* witness? Are you sure you don't want to rethink that?" His voice low as his lips twitch into a sardonic smile.

"But no, that's what I'm saying. I don't think Dani did it. Serena framed her because she was going to expose her! Expose her for *pretending* to be her sister, so she framed her for Josh's murder." My words come out faster now laced with desperation, my throat tightening. "I know this sounds crazy, but just read it, please." I say earnestly.

He exhales slowly, closing the diary with a soft snap.

"Okay, um, I'll look at these." He says his tone softens. "We are having the mother of the victim come to see the body to confirm who is *who*. So, we will be in touch. Get some sleep okay?" he says as if he's concerned about me. *Does he think something is wrong with me?*

I gulp. I don't know if I'm more relieved or horrified that he will read them and find out who *she is*.

41

Karma

ON MY WAY BACK HOME, my mind keeps racing with thoughts about what I should do next. This is making my head hurt. I still believe I can come out on top. Who would believe Serena, now there are so many people against her? Me, her mom, and Dani. I constantly tell myself.

Calming down will make everything okay. I do a breathing exercise I saw on some article, called box breathing. I like it because if you stop breathing, your brain struggles to produce rapid thoughts. Inhale for seven seconds while drawing a line with your fingers, then hold for seven, exhale drawing the top of the box and for seven drawing the bottom then hold for seven seconds to complete the box. And boom, you feel a little less like you want to kill yourself.

After I'm done box breathing, my mind immediately

goes to Brent. He will make me feel better. I get on my phone and text him,

> Hey! Sweet cheeks, are you free tonight?

I giggle, half embarrassed. Hoping he thinks that was funny. I send it as I'm walking down the hall to my room, and then I look up and I see Athena. She peeks her head out of her room as if she was waiting to hear the elevator open. I see her head move from side to side. She swings her eyes at me, and I wave awkwardly as I approach her. Her eyes widen as I get closer and her smile grows wide, and she props up.

"Hey, just the person I wanted to see!" she says in a cheery voice as she takes my hand. Her charm doesn't work now, but she always has this friendly familiar feeling about her. As I look into her eyes, I get a chill down my spine. Am I looking into the eyes of a murderer? A psychopath's eyes, Serena says in the diary that she *knows* she's different. It makes me think if she even cares that she's insane. She acts so casual toward everything.

She senses my distance. Her expression changes immediately, and she tilts her head like a confused dog. Her face hardens and so does her grip on my hand.

"What's wrong with you? Have the cops gotten to you? You know who I am, Karma. Don't you? You know who I am!" she says, demanding an answer. Not breaking eye contact.

"Um, yeah," I say, looking down, taking my hand away. "I'm just tired and all this stuff is stressing me out and I'm traumatized."

"Traumatized? You shouldn't feel that way. You killed someone who was an evil person. You should feel like a hero!" Athena says, still not breaking eye contact. She doesn't know. I'm hesitant to tell her. It's better that she finds out on her own. I nod and smile. She looks at me. With eyes that are not at all kind anymore. It's as if she's threatening me, by contemplating getting rid of me, giving me this eerie feeling in my stomach. I better get myself together.

Brent texts back. It lets out a loud ding thank God. I put my phone out and tell her I have to go.

"Be careful Karma, be careful," she says.

I shoot her a smile and speed walk toward the elevator. I read his text.

"Yes, now I am. Detective Kuang just left my house. You wouldn't guess what he had to say."

42

Karma a week later

ATHENA'S MOM identified who was in the hospital. She says it's Serena Drakos. I'm not sure I can believe her mother, she's not the most *dependable* person. But I thought that's who I shot, but I wasn't sure. They are truly a hard board cut-out copy of each other. I think what really sold it for me was the recognition I sensed in her eyes. And that she said my name first and her sister just echoed.

I feel oddly proud of myself that I finally got her back. They said the machine is what's keeping her alive. Maybe I could-. No, that would be too much of a coincidence. But how would I be able to be incognito in the hospital? I have to sign in and all the cameras... Stop. I can't think like that! Gosh, she really has ruined my life.

The detective told Brent about my fake Instagram account and asked me about it. I lied. Not sure he believes me. I told him that Katherine has always hated me and she's a liar and a bully. The detective remembered me going to Brent's house. He assumed we were an item and wanted to see if the messages online sounded like me, to Lucas. They do, but doesn't every girl sound the same when they like a guy? He said he believes me, but now he looks at me differently and it makes my heart hurt. I can't hide that part of my life anymore. It's borderline violating. That was my business, and I wanted to stop using that Anastasia account. I tried to stop. Lucas wouldn't let me and then he attacked me.

I should tell Brent what really happened. He would surely feel bad for me. That man is no victim. He tried to kill me in cold blood. I have done nothing that bad, intentionally. Never.

I haven't seen Athena in a while. I want to visit Serena to see how she's really doing? Will that make me seem sympathetic or suspicious? I don't know anymore. I heard she was in a coma and being held like a criminal.

Since Athena has come back to work. Well, the real Athena pretending to be Serena that was pretending to be Athena. Everyone is acting like she is some hero survivor. They put up a welcome back Athena banner and are treating her like a poor sick baby. Not the same treatment for me at all. I'm still treated like a peasant. Kendall was talking to me about it.

"I can't believe her sister would do that. It's so crazy. I know that's so hurtful. I heard Athena tried to make up with her by letting her stay at her place, but her sister was just on drugs and a prostitute and stole money from her and everything. It's so sad."

I don't say anything. I don't want to make myself sound bad. "Where did you hear this?" I say curiously.

"That's what everyone is saying. Karen told me. I want to ask Athena, but I know it's not a good time. I don't want to pry, you know. She's so brave."

"Brave? I'm the one who stopped her sister from killing her!" I say defensively. Kendall shoots me a weird look and says she's going to check in with Athena. If anyone's a hero it's me. I don't know why I feel offended. I think it's because everyone's treating this girl like she is a princess. If they only knew.

I try to watch Athena, focusing on her body language and the way she walks. I never have a good view of her walking to check if she's pigeon-toed. Something I've never noticed before, now gives me something to count on. I even beckoned her to come toward me from her desk, but I couldn't get a good view of her feet. Once she's in front of me.

"What are you doing after work?" I ask

"Why?" She says plainly.

I stutter, "Um, just to um, like hangout, catch up. See how you're doing?"

She gives me a brief smile. "Yeah, I can't because my dad is coming to town."

My ears shoot up, her father? The killer/con man?

"Oh, I don't mind. Meeting him would be great. I'm

down to do anything, really. I just need to get out of my room. It's driving me crazy."

She furrows her eyebrows and tilts her head then shrugged.

"Okay sure you can come by, see you around seven," she says then walks away spinning on her heels.

Athena texts me that the plans have changed. The hospital called to tell her that Serena has woken up from her coma, and now they are allowed to visit her. I tell her I will come to support her.

Today is the day I will know who is who. She says okay and for me to just meet them there. Once I get to the hospital, I tell them I'm here with the Drakos family. A nurse escorts me to Serena's room. As we approach, I see Athena and her father standing beside the bed, speaking with the doctor.

From behind, Athena's father cuts an impressive figure, he is every bit the archetype of a silver fox. At 6'2", he towers over Athena, lean and athletic, with wavy salt-and-pepper hair that brushes his ears. He's dressed sharply in dark gray slacks, a black dress shirt, and black loafers. When I walk in, he turns to me, his polite smile revealing a calm yet commanding presence.

"Hello, you must be Karma. My daughter has told me a lot about you." extending his hand I shake it at a loss for words. I nod and smile back. Athena turns to me and thanks me for coming.

"No problem. I know this is awful. I'm sorry." She takes my hand and nods at me. The doctor continues his explanation, and my gaze shifts to the girl lying in the bed. Serena. Her eyes wide but her face falls flat like the rest of her body.

"She's fully cognizant from what we gathered," the doctor explains. "The bullet caused complete paralysis, sparing only her eye movement. For now, we're exploring communication through blinking—using the alphabet if necessary. The police were here earlier, but she was reluctant to cooperate. She wouldn't even look at them." He glances at Serena then back at me, his expression curious.

I follow his gaze. She's looking directly at me. Her eyes wide, blinking rapidly.

"Maybe now she is in the mood." The doctor grabs the alphabet and tells her the rules.

"Okay, when you want me to pick the letter I'm pointing at, wink at that letter. After you wink, I will then start back at the beginning of the alphabet for the following letter, okay blink twice if you understand," the doctor says. She blinks twice, her eyes focused and deliberate. She winks and spells out,

"A-N-A-S-T-A-S-I-A-I-S-H-E-R-E." Then he asks who, and she spells my name. That is Serena Drakos in that bed, now I'm certain. I can tell by the sense of recognition in her eyes, it's the *Athena* I know.

"She is only saying that because she saw it on the news here. And is trying to blame me because she's mad I made her disabled! She was trying to KILL her sister, and this isn't the first time. I already told the detective!" my words spill out in a frantic rush, but the room falls into a stunned silence. Athena and her father are looking at me like I've completely lost my mind.

"I'm sorry," I mumble. Feeling the heat of their judgment. "This has been a lot. I have been holding all this in, because it's an ongoing case. I found these diaries of hers, it's scary she has done a lot of bad things. And she's trying to do everything she can to continue her evil behavior." I feel like they're not believing me. They are still shooting me these bizarre looks, even the doctor.

"Sorry, guys, I have to go. Sorry. Nice to meet you". I say to the dad as I walk out. While I walk toward the subway, I replay what happened in my mind. I think they understood a little, maybe at the end when I started crying. For a woman, it's better to cry when you're mad than to yell. Less crazy lady, more sad grieving lady, goes over better. I hope they don't think I'm crazy. It doesn't matter because I think *they* are crazy. It's even more crazy how Serena got Athena's personality to a T. I'm impressed. I'm not sure if I should pretend that she's my friend and talk to her about everything.

Well, she knows I read the diaries. So, she knows I know. I look at my phone. I have a text from Brent.

Hey

Do you want to come over and talk?

I look up to see when I should get off and see that his stop is next. Wow, what a coincidence. I text him,

> Hey, yes I'm in the area I could be there in like ten minutes.

Okay, see you then.

It only takes me like three minutes to walk to his place. But I need to rehearse what I'm going to say. I knock on his door with a knot in my stomach.

He shoots me a forced smile and steps back to let me in. I sit on the couch and I try to look around and see if any other woman has been in here. He hasn't hung out with me in a week. I thought we were over, but I have too much pride to ask. He asks me how my day was and I lie and say it was good. He takes a deep breath and says,

"So, what's going on, Karma? This still isn't making any sense to me. The detective keeps asking me about you possibly being that woman that used those fake pictures and murdered the boy, Lucas?" he says in a disgusted tone. I fight back tears.

"I told you it's that girl Katherine from high school. She hates me and she even admitted to hacking into that account. Katherine's weird, she's probably behind it all. Katherine bullied me because she found out that me and her boyfriend kissed at her birthday party. It was a mistake, but she never forgave me. I had to move to online school because the bullying got so bad," I say.

He shakes his head, running a hand through his dark curly hair as his eyes narrow at me. "The detective showed me more texts; they sound just like you." His tone was low, almost cold.

I huff defensively. "Don't most young girls sound the same when they like a boy? Like? Flirting?" I say, shrugging my shoulders.

He leans forward curiously. "Okay, yeah, but what were you doing that night?" he says, his eyes boring into mine.

I roll my eyes dramatically, my hand gesturing wildly as I fire back, "Did you bring me here to interrogate me? Who do you think you are? You're no saint your damn self, what about all those fake IDs you made for minors, so they can go out and possibly get hurt, roofied or drunk drive?" My voice rises, the anger mingling with hurt.

He sinks down into the couch beside me, his expression softens and he exhales slowly. "Okay, that's not the same at all, but okay I get it. Sorry, it just really freaked me out. I just had to ask you. I don't think you had anything to do with it. I'm just trying to understand. I believe you. Okay?" His tone becomes gentle, apologetic. As he reaches out and takes my hand, I instinctively pull back.

I swallow hard, my voice trembling as I reply. "I really just didn't like your tone, and I felt like you were antagonizing me and taking someone else's side. When you don't know them," I sniffle, my eyes darting away as I try to hold back the swell of my emotion.

"I know, I know I'm sorry. I didn't mean to. All this stuff is driving me crazy. Are you okay?" he asks softly, his eyes searching mine for reassurance.

I muster a weak smile and shrug. "I guess I'm fine. I'm

still breathing," I say my voice barely above a whisper, as I try to convince both him and myself.

Brent chuckles, and I can't help but laugh too. His smile makes me feel so warm and seen. He then pulls me into a hug. We kiss, then our bodies melt into each other. He takes me to his room. All I can think of is how much I missed this—missed him. As he undresses me, trailing kisses across my skin, the world behind me fades. In his arms, nothing else matters. For a while, everything feels okay again.

The next day at work. I try to avoid Athena. It's so ironic that she is pretending to be Serena, pretending to be herself. She is doing it seamlessly. I guess it's easy when someone has mimicked you their whole life. The only crack in her performance comes when she 'forgets' things and blames it on the 'PTSD' from everything she suffered.

I successfully keep my distance from her, until I walk into the bathroom. She's there, standing at the mirror, fixing her lipstick. When she notices me, she pauses for a second, as if she's choosing her words carefully. I smile politely and book it for the stall. She stops me before I can open the stall door.

"Hey um, I just wanted to say you did the right thing. Everything's on the table now, so we can have a fresh start. I'm sorry about everything she did," she says, smiling softly. Her words catch me off guard. I can't help but notice—again—how much she looks like Serena. It's uncanny. They have the same piercing blue eyes, auburn hair, and smile. I remind myself that they are not even twins, just ten months apart. A genuine smile spreads across my face as I nod.

"No, I'm sorry. It's unbelievable what you've been through and thank you for saying that. I really appreciate it," I say. She smiles at me, her expression warm and sincere, as she leaves.

I feel an immense weight lifted from my shoulders. I heard they put Serena into a home and she's still awaiting sentencing. It feels surreal that this is where things ended up. The final pick is today for our spot at Introspection. I should be excited, but I don't know if I want it anymore. This life here isn't what I imagined it would be. I don't know if I'm cut out for it.

43

Karma a year later

SERENA GOT SENTENCED to twenty-five to life for the murder of Dani's mother, fifty counts of fraud and abuse of the elderly. Officials are holding Serena in a home for the disabled, but they are keeping her in solitary confinement. The judge granted Dani a retrial because Serena is now considered a probable suspect. Athena has agreed to testify against her sister.

We all made it as agents at Introspection, but in different sectors. Brent got assigned to sports ads, Athena to retail ads, and I got put in tech. Athena and I hardly talk anymore. I think I remind her too much of what happened. I don't mind, because the feeling is mutual. Still whenever we pass each other at work events, we exchange polite smiles.

Oddly enough, I kind of miss Serena in some weird way. She was really fun to be around. One day, I bought flowers and went to visit her. When I walked in her room, she wouldn't even look at me. All I could see were the tears streaming silently down her cheeks.

Brent and I have been living together for the past year. After the internship ended, so did the free housing. We never really discussed it, it sort of just happened. I started staying over every night, then at some point, all my clothes ended up at his place, miraculously. It feels natural though, like this is where I'm supposed to be.

Today we went out after work at our boss's house to celebrate the deal we secured with Apple. His house is enormous, a mansion. I had a few drinks to get through the rest of the night. But Brent is in his element, mingling, chatting effortlessly with everyone. Watching him work the room, I couldn't help but admire how good he is at this, but I couldn't bear to talk to another soul. I walk to Brent and tap him on the shoulder.

"Hey babe I'm ready to go. I'm tired and my feet hurt," I say, pouting.

He places his hand on my shoulder and kisses my cheek, whispering in my ear. "Okay baby, let me say bye to the host. Then we'll leave. Start up the car. I'll only be a minute," he says as he goes to find our boss until he gets stopped by another woman again.

It's so annoying having an attractive, outgoing boyfriend. I trust him though. Well, only as much as I trust the passcode on his phone. I head back to the car and wait. Brent returns a couple minutes later, sliding into the driver's seat with an exasperated sigh.

"Geez, those people are exhausting, nice call leaving early," he says as he backs up the car.

I giggle. "Really? I thought you were having fun?"

"No," he says, shaking his head. "In this industry it's not what you know; it's who you know. These people's husbands and families are probably all rich and I want their money. So, if I have to make my cheeks sore from fake smiling to make my pockets swell, our pockets swell. Then I will do so," he says.

I forget how smart and hardworking he is. That reminds me I need to answer a few emails.

I smile "Hell yeah."

He squeezes my thigh with a grin, and we both laugh.

We make it home and I jump in the shower. He joins me later. Afterward I dry off, put on one of Brent's band tees, go to the couch and pull out my laptop. I start on a few emails and update spreadsheets for the new Apple launch we are working on. Feeling my eyes getting heavy, I grab an energy drink. Brent comes in looking at me with concern.

"When are you coming to bed?"

"In a little. I just have a few loose ends. I need to tie up before the morning," I reply typing away.

At some point, I must have nodded off because I wake up with a blanket draped over me and my laptop sitting open on the coffee table. I look at the time it's 11:30, I panic. *I overslept.* I call Brent's name, but there is no response. I get up to check the bedroom. I don't see him. Why didn't he wake me? I need to call him, but I can't find my phone.

Frustrated, I flop back on the couch, defeated. *I'm just going to call in sick.* Martha can finish the rest of the groundwork today. I'll assist at home if needed.

Maybe Brent went to get breakfast or something. I reach for my laptop to check my work email, but something catches my eye. The browser is open to my *personal* email account—one I haven't used in years. Confused, I lean closer and see the email that's open. It's from Instagram.

The subject line reads:

"Anastasia, you requested a password change."

My stomach sinks. *Why is this email open? Why is it on this account? Did I do this by accident? No way?* A sickening thought creeps in. *Did Brent do this? But how would he even know about this email?*

I start to panic, heart racing. I call out Brent's name again louder this time. No answer. I rush back to the bedroom and freeze when I see his things are gone.

His clothes. His bags. Everything. My phone is gone too. I go back to the living room and return to my laptop. I open the browser history and see what else was accessed. My heart pounds as I see the web searches for the cold case involving Lucas's murder—searches tied to the picture of the girl I used for the fake Anastasia account.

My head spins.

He *knows.*

44

Athena

I woke up early to go to the county jail. I have been texting Brent on the way about Karma. My sister, Serena is a liar, just enough to get what she wants when it suits her. She is an instant gratification type of girl; she thrives off of it.

Karma's story didn't sit right with me. So, I dug into it. Serena always kept a diary, her most trusted confidant, the only thing she was truly honest with. Her only true friend. *Poor girl.*

It didn't take long for me to crack into her laptop. After a few wrong guesses. I realized the password was: Kyle143.

Of course it was. I wanted to investigate further, but I couldn't do anything too obvious; Karma would suspect me. Brent, however was a different story. She'd never see him coming. I told him everything he needs to know should be in that email. This morning Brent called to tell me he had photographed everything he found and was heading to the police station. He sounded sick about it, poor guy. He's gorgeous though—I'll surely help him get over it. He can rest that pretty head on my shoulder.

When I arrive at the jail, they search me and escort me through the building. I tell them I'm here to see Dani. As I step into the visitor area, she's already seated, waiting for me. We lock eyes and for the first time in what feels forever. I see her—the girl who was *my best friend*. I see a glimmer of recognition in her gaze too. My chest tightens. I can't resist smiling as I pick up the phone.

"I've missed you so much."

About the Author

Destinee Boston is an emerging author of thrillers and mysteries. This is Destinee's debut novel. She is from Oklahoma and has a fiance and two adorable cats.